PRAISE FOR
SLEEP◉VER

"Malone's boisterous whirl of capers, pranks, and mystery deftly contains Meghan's journey of self-discovery."—*Kirkus Reviews*

"Equal parts mystery, caper, and friendship story."—*School Library Journal*

DON'T MISS THESE OTHER
GREAT BOOKS BY JEN MALONE
At Your Service
Best. Night. Ever.

WRITTEN WITH GAIL NALL
You're Invited
You're Invited Too

SLEEP THE OVER

BY JEN MALONE

mix
aladdin

ALADDIN M!X

New York London Toronto Sydney New Delhi

This book is a work of fiction. Any references to historical events, real people, or real places are used fictitiously. Other names, characters, places, and events are products of the author's imagination, and any resemblance to actual events or places or persons, living or dead, is entirely coincidental.

aladdin M!X

ALADDIN M!X

Simon & Schuster Children's Publishing Division

1230 Avenue of the Americas, New York, New York 10020

First Aladdin M!X paperback edition May 2017

Text copyright © 2016 by Jen Malone

Cover illustration copyright © 2016 by Lucy Truman

Also available in an Aladdin hardcover edition.

ALADDIN and related logo are registered trademarks of Simon & Schuster, Inc.

ALADDIN M!X and related logo are registered trademarks of Simon & Schuster, Inc.

For information about special discounts for bulk purchases, please contact Simon & Schuster Special Sales at 1-866-506-1949 or business@simonandschuster.com.

The Simon & Schuster Speakers Bureau can bring authors to your live event.

For more information or to book an event contact the Simon & Schuster Speakers Bureau at 1-866-248-3049 or visit our website at www.simonspeakers.com.

Designed by Laura Lyn DiSiena

The text of this book was set in Dante.

Manufactured in the United States of America 0417 OFF

10 9 8 7 6 5 4 3 2 1

The Library of Congress has cataloged the hardcover edition as follows:

Names: Malone, Jen, author.

Title: The sleepover / by Jen Malone.

Description: First Aladdin hardcover edition. | New York : Aladdin, 2016.

Summary: Four girls have a sleepover but awaken to find a big mess and no memory of how it all happened.

Identifiers: LCCN 2015050808 | ISBN 9781481452618 (hardcover) | ISBN 9781481452625 (eBook)

Subjects: | CYAC: Sleepovers—Fiction.

Classification: LCC PZ7.M29642 Sl 2016 | DDC [Fic] dc23

ISBN 9781481452601 (pbk)

TO CAROLINE
MAY ALL YOUR SLEEPOVERS BE TAME
IN COMPARISON

SLEEPTHEOVER

PART ONE

PART ONE

CHAPTER ONE

The Promise of Epic

Tonight is gonna be EPIC.

I smile to myself and work in a few hip wiggles in time to the song blaring (or at least nudged to the highest possible volume I can get away with without my mom appearing in my doorway with her arms crossed), as I toss my favorite polka-dot flannel pajama bottoms into my bag. I have to stop dancing to wrestle my pillow into my already jam-packed sleeping bag pouch, and then I jump in place to get the drawstring to close. Who knew packing for a sleepover could be such a workout?

My hand hovers over Hippy, my stuffed hippo, lying face-down on my comforter. Pack him. No, don't. Yes, do. No, way too babyish. This might be my first sleepover, but I'm not actually *that* young. Depending on whether you consider twelve and three-quarters young. (FYI: I don't.) And, well, it isn't technically my first sleepover, but it *is* the first one where I fully and completely intend to make it to the actual sleeping-over part. Let's just say there was a little *Could you please, please call my mom to pick me up?* incident when it came to lights-out at my friend's house when I was seven. It, um, might have happened again at age eight. And nine. We sort of skipped trying after that, but I'm (almost, in three months) *thirteen* now.

I can do this.

I pause with one hand on the zipper of my duffel bag. Then I reach across it, grab Hippy, wrap him in my West Oak Middle School sweatshirt, and nestle the bundle gently underneath the clothes I've packed to change into in the morning.

Epic is epic, but *if* we ever get around to actual sleeping at this sleepover, a girl might need her stuffed hippo. I'm just saying.

I shake my bag to clear space for a few extras.

- ✔ Nail polish "borrowed" from Mom's bathroom: check

- ✔ Camera for maximum selfie-taking (even if I'll have to connect it to a computer to put the pictures on Anna Marie's Instagram since *someone's* parents don't approve of either smartphones or social media sites for not-yet-teenagers): check.

- ✔ *Girls' Life* magazine, latest issue: check.

I pull my iPod from its dock and tuck it on top before zipping my duffel closed. Done! Nope, not done. I open it again to slide three fair-trade organic carob bars (despite Mom's claims, these are *not* "practically the next best thing to a candy bar"—don't be fooled) along the side. *Zzzzip!*

There. I hoist the sleeping bag over my shoulder and try to ignore the fact that the strap is digging into my skin. You know what? I don't even care. Nothing is going to ruin tonight!

Epic. It's gonna be epic. I don't know *exactly* what that means, but Paige and Anna Marie keep saying they want my first true sleepover to be epic and it sounds like a good thing and I'm just going to pretend I don't have the teensy, tiniest, little belly-flip feeling when I try to picture the night. It might be true that I've never been an epic kind of person, but who's to say I couldn't be if I tried? And when better to try than tonight?

The doorbell rings out Pachelbel's "Canon in D" in tinny ding-dong notes.

"Mom! *Mo-ooom!* Can you get that? It's Paige!" I yell down to the first level. She hates when I yell between floors, but I know Paige, and she'll be leaning on that doorbell again in 2.5 seconds. Mom will hate that even more, I'm positive.

I take the stairs from my attic bedroom two at a time and thud onto the second-floor landing. Leaning over the railing, I spot my mom in the downstairs hallway, one arm in a cardigan sweater and the other grabbing at the air behind her for the empty sleeve. The doorbell chimes again, followed by three short bursts as Paige jabs the button.

Knew it.

"Someone needs to teach that girl some manners. She's murdering Pachelbel," Mom mutters loudly enough for me to hear as I reach the bottom stair. Tugging the door open, Mom raises an eyebrow at Paige, looking oh-so-Paige with her long blond hair in waves and wearing a fringed denim miniskirt and furry boots. She has her elbow propped on the doorframe.

"Mrs. A. What up?"

"Paige." Just the one word, but I can hear all the disapproval it holds. I cringe and hope my friend doesn't pick up on it. I hurry to cross the hallway, dragging my duffel behind me, and insert myself in front of my mom. Luckily, Paige just smiles her normal grin at me and blows her bangs out of her eyes.

"Girlfriend! You ready for an awesomesauce night?"

I start to bounce a little in excitement, but then I remember Mom just behind me.

"Um, yeah, it should be good." I shrug and kick at the door threshold with my sneaker. With my shoulders angled so Mom can't see my face, I catch Paige's eyes and send her a silent plea to play it cool.

I turn to my mother with a small smile and see her eyes narrow slightly. "I fail to see what's 'awesomesauce' about working on a science fair project. You have your biology textbook in there, right, Meghan Elizabeth?"

I shoot another desperate look at Paige, but I know she'll catch on. She has two older brothers and an older sister, so she's well schooled in the art of parental management. She doesn't even miss a beat before she says, "No worries. She can use mine, Mrs. A. I only meant that plotting the nocturnal exercise patterns of Anna Marie's hamster has the potential to be totally amazeballs when we take first place in the science fair, is all."

My mother does not look convinced. It's not that Mom wouldn't let me go on a regular sleepover without the whole science fair story, but then I'd have to listen to all kinds of lectures on what to do . . . and what not to do. It's not worth it. Plus, with my personal sleepover history, it's *really* not worth it. Mom's eyebrows do that meet-in-the-middle-like-a-V thing above her nose, and she shakes her head once.

"You have your retainer? And your Ladybug cell in case of an emergency? And please go to bed at a reasonable time, you hear me? We're going right from picking you up tomorrow afternoon to handbell rehearsal at church, and I don't want you yawning your way through it, or Reverend Robbins will be offended. And for heaven's sake, Meghan, don't forget to floss!"

Paige is one of my good friends, so she knows this is how it is, but yeah . . . my parents are pretty strict. (Well, mostly Mom, but Dad doesn't like to "rock the boat" once Mom's made up her mind about something.) You would think living under martial rule would have made me desperate to get away for all those other sleepovers, but the thing is, Mom's also got a pretty overactive imagination, and I think maybe I inherited it. Usually what happens when she won't let me walk to the park alone because of "stranger danger" or warns me against eating anything with Yellow 5 dye in it because she watched a talk show that said it could cause cancer, is that I end up not even really wanting to because who wants to be kidnapped or to get sick? Not me.

It's just lately I've been starting to wonder if maybe Mom's a little *too* overprotective.

I mean, I know she is (says the only girl on the soccer field wearing a bike helmet).

I guess maybe what I'm actually starting to wonder is if I'm still okay with it. Tonight's kind of a test. If I can have fun and go a little bit crazy and nothing bad happens, maybe I need to work up the courage to talk to Mom about a few things. And, duh, what could ever go wrong at a simple sleepover at my best friend's house, where I spend practically half my time anyway?

I give Mom a quick hug and say, "Sure thing. Floss.

Retainer. Call. Got it. Say good night to Dad for me." I readjust my sleeping bag and drag my duffel around Mom's planted legs. Paige backs off the step and onto the path, smiling angelically at my mother. With her pale blond waves, she really does look like an angel.

"Enjoy your evening, Mrs. A." Under her breath as we walk away she mutters, "Dude, *what* is a Ladybug cell?"

I groan and whisper, "It's a starter cell phone. With a total of two buttons: home and 9-1-1."

Paige snorts a giggle and grabs the duffel out of my hands as we make our way toward her sister in the waiting car. I steal a glance behind me at Mom because I'm positive she won't let me drive off with a college kid behind the wheel, but she's already closed the door. Phew!

"Oh, my poor sheltered Meghan," Paige says when she catches my worried look. "You're not going to know what hit you. Mark my words, Megs. Tonight? Is gonna be *EPIC*."

It doesn't exactly inspire confidence in our best-night-ever plans when the birthday girl can't answer the door because she's arguing with her mother. Maybe *arguing* isn't the right word, but it's definitely a Serious Discussion, and I feel totally weird ringing the doorbell in the middle of it. The door itself is propped open a few inches and, technically, we could just walk in, which Anna Marie's mom always tells me I should do since I'm here so much, but then we would be interrupting and it would be all awkward and . . .

I steal a glance at Paige, who just shrugs and plops down on the step. It takes a lot to make Paige uncomfortable, which probably mostly has to do with the older siblings thing. At Paige's house, chaos and bickering are everyday occurrences, unlike at my house, which is always dust-free and orderly and church-quiet except for when Dad plays his cello.

"But it's *my* birthday. Shouldn't I get a say in this?" Anna Marie is saying, kind of high-pitched and pleadinglike.

"Bug, I know it's not ideal," her mom answers. "But your father asked a special favor, and I think it's a reasonable request. You're already skipping out on your annual sunrise birthday hike up Mount Ellis with him."

Mrs. Guerrero's voice is gentle, just like she is. I love, love, LOVE Anna Marie's mom. She's warm and soft and always just a little frazzled. It's not like I don't love my own parents most of all because—*obviously*—of course I do. I just wish sometimes they could relax a little more, especially my mother.

Okay, I've held out on something I've been dying to do for long enough. I can't take it anymore! I steal the tiniest of peeks at the house next door, just like I do every time I'm at Anna Marie's. I can't even help it. It's like there's a magnet attached to my head and the other magnet is on Jake Ribano's house.

It's so not fair that Anna Marie gets to live next door

to Jake, the cutest guy in our grade and, also, kind of the scariest. Well, not scary exactly; it's just that he's a little bit of a rebel. Seeing as how I am the exact polar opposite of a rebel, it makes him sort of fascinating. At least that's what I'm blaming my stalkerish tendencies on. Not the fact that he's got this floppy blue-black hair he's always pushing out of his eyes absentmindedly or anything shallow like that. Totally involuntarily, my heart speeds up a little at the thought of catching a glimpse of him.

But no.

His house is dark and quiet. My heartbeat slows and steadies.

Inside, Mrs. Guerrero says, "Besides, in a few months, Veronica's going to be part of this family whether you like it or not. And I can promise you, your life will be a lot easier if you learn to deal with that."

"Mom. Seriously. You've met Veronica. She's a freak!" Anna Marie is practically shouting now, and I cringe and avoid looking at Paige. So mega-awkward. I feel extra bad for my best friend. I can't even imagine having a stepsister forced on me, and Anna Marie already has her hands full with a bratty little brother, Max. I used to beg my parents for a baby brother or sister until I realized I could end up with a Max. No, thanks.

"Anna Marie! That's no way to talk about someone who

will be family soon. You have to find a way past this, prefera-bly before Dad's wedding."

Mrs. Guerrero's voice gets quieter, and both Paige and I scoot our butts a little bit closer to the doorway, exchanging guilty glances as we do. "Look," Mrs. G. says. "I'll admit Veronica has some . . . oddities. But she seems like a sweet enough girl, and you're the same age, so you have something in common right there. You can't argue she hasn't been doing her part to try to get to know you, and I just think you *could* meet her halfway."

Anna Marie snorts loud enough that we can hear it. "I don't consider charting my horoscope based on the latitude and longitude of my birth location 'getting to know me.'"

Paige stuffs her fist into her mouth to keep from laughing, and I elbow her. The only thing worse than interrupting would be getting busted eavesdropping. Paige rubs at her elbow and mouths, *Ow!*

I ignore her.

Inside, Anna Marie's mom sounds sympathetic. "I know it's your big sleepover party and this is getting sprung on you at the last minute. But I'm trying to be supportive of Dad's decision to remarry, and I think allowing Veronica to be part of your birthday would be a really nice gesture. Okay, sweets?"

Anna Marie sighs. "Not really. But I'm guessing this is a rhetorical question."

"She'll be here in a half hour. I expect you to be inclusive. It means a lot to Dad *and* to me."

It's quiet then, and after about ten seconds Paige pops to her feet and puts her hand out to help me up. Together we lean on the doorbell and wait for Anna Marie to fling the door open the rest of the way.

CHAPTER TWO

Pineapple-and-Pickle Pizza

"Squeeeeeeeeeeeee!"

I'm pretty sure we just woke up people sleeping in Australia, but so what? It's finally here! The party is starting! We scramble inside, knocking bags and hips as we barrel down the basement stairs.

I don't mention a single thing about the fight we overheard, and neither does Paige. Anna Marie seems okay, and why ruin a good sleepover with serious talk? Paige drops her backpack and sleeping bag at the base of the stairs, forcing me to leap from the last step over the discarded gear. I swallow a sigh and move her stuff against the wall, where it won't be a safety hazard.

Oh my God. I'm turning into my mother. It's official. I may need medical attention.

"I. Am. So. *Excited!*" Anna Marie yells. "Omigosh, you guys, tonight was taking forever to get here even though it's not technically tonight yet because it's only five o'clock, but you know what I mean. I'm so, so glad I overruled Mom about the party starting now, because we need the extra time to do all the fun stuff before we get tired, and if you start a sleepover at seven or something, then you barely get to do anything before you have to go to sleep, although we're totally not going to sleep, are we? I want to see how late we can stay up! I say two a.m., but I couldn't make myself nap earlier when I tried, so I bet I crash by midnight. And don't worry, Megs, we'll stay up all night with you if that's what it takes so you aren't freaked out. Omigosh, you're *heeeeere!*"

Anna Marie . . . likes to talk. A lot. Sometimes this is a good trait in a best friend, like on days you're really sleepy because your math homework took forever the night before, or you're distracted looking for a certain neighbor of hers in the hallway between classes, and sometimes it's a little bit annoying. Right now? It's perfect! Her excitement is way contagious.

She grabs us both by the hands, and we all jump in place. I don't know why this gives us the major giggles, but it does. I laugh at how Anna Marie's short, spiky hair barely moves with her jumps. I have no idea what my ponytail is doing and, for once, I don't care. I don't even care about all those tiny doubts I had in the back of mind every time I pictured this party, worrying about whether I'd have to call my mom to pick me up because I was too big of a baby to spend the entire night. At the moment they're all just . . . gone. Poof.

"Okay, what's first? Snacks? Spa Night? Xbox?" Anna Marie asks, waving her hands around the open room. I've spent so much time in this basement, I could probably even find my way around it blindfolded. On the center wall is an oversize flat-screen TV with a cabinet below it. Without looking, I can guarantee there are cords from the Xbox in a tangled mess on the floor in front of it. The couch is this big tan sectional with lumpy cushions in the middle of the space, and behind it is a Ping-Pong table and a wood bar Anna Marie's dad decorated with signs from Irish pubs, back when he still lived here and called the basement his "man cave."

"Presents!" Paige declares. We've only been here for 2.5 seconds but, clearly, Paige cannot wait one more instant to give Anna Marie whatever it is she got her. She yanks her backpack from next to the wall where I'd nudged it and rifles through until she finds a rectangular-shaped box tied with purple (Anna Marie's favorite color) ribbon.

Paige's grin is huge as she hands the package over, and her smile grows even bigger as Anna Marie tugs off the ribbon and unwraps the paper. Anna Marie holds up the cellophane-wrapped Summer Dance Party 11 for Xbox and squeals.

"Every party needs dancing!" Paige declares.

Anna Marie throws her arms around Paige and says, "It's perfect! Thank you so much! I was getting really good at all the songs on SDP 10, and that's awesome but also kind of boring, ya know? And now I'll have a whole ton of new ones to learn. Yay! I love it so much!"

Geez, I hope she likes the journal I bought her as much. Writing quietly is not exactly a party activity, and now I'm worried I should have brought something more fun. I know Anna Marie will like it, because we're alike in most ways and I have to put all my thoughts on paper or it's like they never happened (and let's be honest, Anna Marie always has a *lot* to say about anything and everything), but this party is supposed to be all about letting loose and coming out of my shell. Maybe that means I should have found something we all could have had fun with tonight, like Paige's present. Why am I such a fail at party guesting? At the very least, I'm waiting until later to give Anna Marie my present.

Paige has dropped to her knees and is pushing the bulky coffee table tight against the couch, clearing an open space in the middle of the carpet, and Anna Marie is sliding the game into the console. I grab a controller to help out.

"'Maniac' or 'Funkytown'?" I ask, scrolling my thumb along the buttons.

"'American Boy,'" orders Paige. "It's Kanye!"

I'm not supposed to listen to Kanye. Mom doesn't like "the way those rap singers disrespect women." But I don't mention this. Instead I find the song and hit play before jumping back up and joining Paige and Anna Marie in a line. Of course

Paige, who is allowed to do, watch, and listen to anything on account of being the youngest child by a whole lot of years, knows every word. At least it doesn't take me long to learn the refrain, and the dance moves come pretty naturally.

I'm paying so much attention to the scores on the screen and trying to beat my friends that I don't notice the girl with stringy hair clutching the banister and bobbing her head along until she sings out (off tune, I might add), "'Take me to New York. I'd like to see LA.'"

Paige and Anna Marie spin around, and I'm so startled I drop my controller.

"'I really want to come kick it with you,' the girl continues, squinting through thick glasses at the lyrics on the screen and emphasizing them with a karate-style leg move that causes her to tumble down the last two stairs and land on her hands and knees.

The song ends as all three of us gape at the girl in front of us on the floor. If it were me sprawled there, I would have practically died, but this girl seems completely *un*embarrassed. In fact, she's *smiling*.

"Hi, everyone!"

Anna Marie sighs, walks to the steps, and reaches out a hand to help the girl up.

"Guys, this is my, um . . . This is Veronica. She's, uh, she's joining us tonight."

Anna Marie has one of those forced-polite smiles that's exactly like the one I plaster on at coffee hour after church when all the old ladies pet my arm and ask me if I have a boyfriend yet. (Answer I give: No, I'm still too young for that. Answer I'd like to give: No, and haven't you ever heard of women's lib? Girls these days have way more to do with their time than think about boys, you know. *Actual* answer: No, but I definitely wouldn't complain if I did and, please, God, could it be Jake Ribano?)

I exchange a quick glance with Paige behind Anna Marie's back, and try to make my smile more genuine as I say, "Um, hey, Veronica. It's nice to meet you."

Just because I've heard Anna Marie complain nonstop about her weird stepsister-to-be doesn't mean I have to judge her before I know her. Although there's probably some kind of Best Friend Code that says I do. But still.

Paige also allows a small smile and then turns her attention back to queuing up the next song.

"So, what are you guys doing?" Veronica asks.

Um, isn't it obvious? But no, that's mean.

I keep my voice upbeat and answer, "We're just playing a dance game. Do you want to use my remote? I can sit this one out." Even if I wanted to, I can't turn off the manners Mom and Dad always insist on. And I *don't* want to. I'm not rude.

Veronica adjusts the strap on her ruffled tank top, which

she's layered *over* a gray sweatshirt. Her jeans are baggy and sag at the knees.

"Oh, that's okay," she answers. "I can use the time to set up my sleeping area. I have a cot to assemble and an air mattress I have to blow up, and Mom said it was okay to bring a folding camping table to put my alarm clock and my water bottle on. Oh, but someone has to remind me, I'm only allowed to fill that up once because otherwise I'll wet the bed. Not to worry, though, because I borrowed an adult diaper from my grams, so I'll pop that on before we go to sleep either way. I'm totally prepared for tonight. Speaking of which, did any of you bring your tarot cards? If you didn't, that's okay. I brought extras, but some people are pretty particular about using their own decks, know what I mean?"

Paige's eyebrows reach her hairline, and I just know she's biting the inside of her cheek to keep from smiling, because her eyes start to water a little. I kick her (subtly) and aim a *Be nice!* look her way, which makes her roll her eyes.

"Um, I don't have my own tarot cards," I say. "But, you know, I've always been curious about them. Maybe later you can show us how they work."

Anna Marie mouths a *thank-you* at me, and I smile. She gestures to a clear space behind the Ping-Pong table and says to Veronica, "If you want to set up there for now, you can."

"Oh, that looks perfect. Hey, do you think there are any spiders in this basement? I love spiders. Oooh look, the light over there will make a perfect nightlight so I can read my comics if I have trouble sleeping. If any of you guys know what happens in the latest volume of *Get Fuzzy*, I'm serious, *do not* tell me. I can't wait to find out if Bucky Katt and Satchel Pooch finally become friends in this one. Really, truly, *don't* tell me."

Veronica makes a threatening face and points her finger at each of us, as if expecting one of us to blurt out a spoiler to a comic book I can guarantee none of us have ever heard of, much less read.

"We'll try to contain ourselves," Paige says, rolling her eyes again and turning back to the television. Thankfully, I'm pretty sure Veronica doesn't get sarcasm, because she just smiles brightly and chirps, "Thanks!" before pacing out the spot she has in mind for her cot.

She wastes no time lugging something that looks like a second Ping-Pong table (this one folded over) down the steps and opening it on its side to reveal an army-green camping cot. Dropping to her knees, she yanks each leg open until the contraption looks like one of those fainting goats, post faint. Anna Maria sighs and circles behind the sofa to grab an end so she can help Veronica turn it right side up. I feel like I should be trying to help too, but all I can do is stare, my mouth open.

Veronica does this kind of bobbing thing with her head as she examines the cot, then she pats the fabric a few times with her hand before turning her back to it and plopping down butt first. She bounces a bunch of times.

"This'll do. Time for the air mattress-pump. AM, you got a place I can plug in the pump to blow it up?"

I cringe. Anna Marie goes crazy whenever anyone tries to give her a nickname. Even leaving off the Marie part and just calling her Anna makes her nutso. Last year we had a substitute teacher during the whole time Mrs. McClusky was off having her baby, and Anna Marie refused to answer anytime the woman addressed her as Anna. It got to the point where the sub asked for a conference with Mrs. Guerrero, who set her straight by saying, "I support Anna Marie's actions. In fact, if I wanted my daughter to be called Anna, I would have named her that."

Actually, Mrs. Guerrero's pet name for Anna Marie— Bug—is the only other thing I've ever seen Anna Marie tolerate.

My best friend looks ready to respond, but in the end she purses her lips and points to the closest wall outlet. A quiet Anna Marie is something I never thought I'd live to see.

Paige and I pretend to be busy scrolling through song selections on the Summer Dance Party game, but ultimately we come right back to "American Boy." It's too good not to have another go at it.

Just as soon as the air mattress–pump noise ends.

"I hope you're decent, ladies," comes a singsong voice hidden by the staircase. A video camera appears through the railing of the steps and swivels to capture the action—ha, as if there's anything to capture—in the basement. Blergh. I'd know that voice anywhere. It haunts my nightmares.

"*GET OUT*, you freak!" Anna Marie screams. "*Mooooooom!*"

The camera snakes back through the railing, and a second later Anna Marie's little brother, Max, appears, a giant grin on his freckled face and two hands in the air. He's worked for ten years to achieve Perfect Brat status, and let's just say, mission: accomplished.

"Chillax, sis. Mom sent me down to tell you the pizza is here," he says.

Anna Marie throws an Xbox remote at his head, but he's had years of practice ducking it, so it goes whirring right over his shoulder and smacks against the wall.

"This *BETTER* be the last we see of you tonight, Max!" Anna Marie threatens.

"Whatevs," Max answers, clomping back up the steps.

Anna Marie takes a deep breath and glances at each of us. She seems embarrassed, but it's not like we don't get it. . . . Max is a terror. I know it, and Paige knows it too. Maybe not Veronica yet, but if she's joining the family, it won't take long. Anna Marie shakes it off and smiles. "Okay, who's hungry?"

Veronica drops the air mattress pump, vaults around the Ping-Pong table, and races for the steps. "Me, me! Ooh, I really hope your mom ordered one with pineapple and pickles! It's my favorite kind!"

CHAPTER THREE

Zombies at the Drive-In

"Are you guys having so much fun? I'm having so much fun. We should do this every weekend, although I guess then it wouldn't be as fun because it would be normal and not special but—omigosh, who on earth would watch *Zombies at the Drive-In Part Seven*? Does that mean there were really parts one through six?" Anna Marie chatters as Paige flips through the on-demand listings, searching for a suitable horror movie. We're back in the basement, snacks in tow, after polishing off two pizzas between the four of us. (Luckily, neither had so much as a hint of pickles *or* pineapples.)

"*Creepy Baby Dolls Come Alive*?" Paige asks.

I cannot even *believe* I'm actually going to watch a horror movie. I could blame the fact that I've never watched one on my parents, because I know without asking what their answer would be if I said, *Hey, Mom, Dad, so can I check out* Werewolf Apocalypse *before bed tonight?* Um, yeah right.

But my parents aren't here now, and I can't get in trouble, which means the splishy-sploshy churning in my stomach at the mere thought of serial killers in hockey masks or vampires with blood-dripping teeth is all me and makes it pretty clear why I never bothered asking in the first pace. I'm a giant scaredy-cat. *Meow.*

But I'm also the one who wanted the full sleepover experience, and horror movies are practically a requirement. I *promised* myself I wasn't going to get all wimpy tonight. Not tonight. Tonight is about acting different. Acting way more like Paige and way less like boring old Meghan. (I'm putting Anna Marie right in the middle of us, because at least *she's* seen *Ghostbusters*.)

Anna Marie touches my leg. "Are you good with this? It won't, like, make things worse for you at bedtime, right? We want you with us all night, so if there's something we have planned that's gonna change that for you, we're counting on you to tell us, 'kay?"

I force a grin and nod. It won't make things worse. At least I'm pretty sure it won't. I won't let it.

Anna Marie smiles back and then asks, "Did you guys see the commercials for that one with the ghost that gets captured on the family's home-surveillance cameras and it's, like, standing *right* next to the faces of the people who live there while they sleep?" She hugs her arms to her chest. "I swear,

I'd rather die. Shoot me now." She tucks her legs under herself on the couch and lets out a giant whole-body shiver. Then her hand snakes across the cushions to grab a handful of M&M's.

"But ghosts are cool," Veronica says. "I have one that lives in my attic, and sometimes I bring him oatmeal cookies. He can't eat them on account of his being all vapory and stuff, but he says he likes the smell of them."

For the hundredth time that night, Paige, Anna Marie, and I exchange glances above Veronica's head. What would be proper protocol here? Ask about the ghost? Ignore her obviously made-up story?

Paige settles our silent debate when she lets out a giant sigh and tosses the remote onto the couch. "There's nothing good here. Most of these movies are all dumb, but not so bad that they're funny. And the other ones are so legit scary that we need to save them for after midnight for maximum effect. Lame-o."

Anna Marie snatches the remote and flips back to the dance game on the Xbox, letting the soundtrack offer background music. "We could give each other mani-pedis. I bought stick-on designs. Or my mom got us cookie dough. We could bake cookies and not let my bratty brother have a single one. He and that weirdo little friend he has over will go ballistic."

"I'm all for cookies," I say, putting the bowl of M&M's aside and standing. Anna Marie's mom always gets the good, nonorganic, non-reduced-sugar kind of cookie dough. I'm betting it probably has preservatives and everything. Which also means it's obscenely awesome.

Paige tucks her knee up and rests her chin on it. "You guys. We need to think bigger. I vowed we'd be off the hook tonight."

I mean, I did too, even if I'm not exactly sure what "off the hook" would look like.

Paige grabs my arm. "You promised me we'd do stuff we'd never do otherwise. For you *and* for me. My brother will *not* shut up about this crazy bachelor party he went to last month, and my sister's sorority just finished Greek Week— you should just hear the stories. I need something equally amazing to wow them with so they'll stop treating me like their ittle, wittle baby sister."

This probably isn't the best time to break it to Paige that being ten years younger than her next-older sibling means she's probably *always* gonna be the baby sister. Instead I chew on my lip for a second before saying, "Well, like, what did you have in mind?"

Veronica says, "What about blindfolded Ping-Pong?"

But Paige is already grinning. Uh-oh. I know that grin. "Let's stalk some guys from school on Instagram. Maybe we could find someone who wants to meet us once your mom goes to bed."

Anna Marie gapes at her. "Paige, we can't sneak out. That's not what I meant by crazy, and you know it."

I nod too.

Paige squints her eyes at me. "We *said* we'd do epic, Megs. What did you expect?"

I don't know what I expected. But not that. Sneaking out is one step shy of illegal. Anna Marie puts a hand on Paige's arm and takes my hand with her other. "You guys. Quit it. No one's sneaking out. There's plenty of other stuff we can do to make it awesome. Besides, it's my birthday, and birthday girl rules say no fighting at my party."

I squeeze Anna Marie's hand, and she passes along the squeeze, like we're little kids back in our Girl Scouts circle singing the "Make New Friends" song at the end of the meeting. All three of us grin, and the tension escapes the room.

"Oh drat. I wish I'd known we were going out later. I would have brought my night-vision goggles," Veronica says.

Our grins freeze on our faces and then melt away like candle wax. We're all looking at Veronica, but only Paige has the nerve to ask, "What do *you* need night-vision goggles for?"

Veronica gives her a look that clearly means *Duh!* and answers, "So I can watch for the Chinese-food delivery guy. It's really cool. I turn off all the lights in my house and stare out the window, and I can see everything perfectly. I know the exact minute he turns onto our street."

"Um, wouldn't the headlights on his car tell you that too?" Paige asks.

Veronica tilts her head and says, "Well, *yeah*, but he turns them off when he parks the car, and this way I can watch him walk the whole way up the path to our door."

Paige's mouth hangs open for a second. After a few blinks, she recovers and gives a little shake of her head. She looks around at each of us before proclaiming, "I know! How about we play I Never?"

"I never what?" I ask.

"It's a game. My sister told me about it, and she plays it all the time in college. We need the M&M's."

I reach across the sofa to retrieve the bowl.

"Okay, how do we play?" asks Anna Marie, sitting cross-legged on the floor next to Paige and bouncing a little. It's good to finally have a plan, and I'm feeling that twinge of excitement again. This game is new and different, and I'm guessing it's superfun if Paige's sister taught it to her.

"So, we take turns," Paige says, "and each of us says something we've never done before. Like a statement. It could be all, 'I never . . . jumped off the high dive at the pool,' or whatever. And then anyone in the circle who *has* done it eats an M&M, and if someone hasn't done it, she doesn't eat anything."

"I'm scared of the low dive, but the high dive doesn't bother me," says Veronica, cracking open a can of Mountain Dew.

She wiggles the metal tab on top until it snaps loose and then reaches across to untie Anna Marie's sneaker. She threads the tab through the shoelace and then reties the laces. "There you go. Happy birthday."

"Um, thanks?" Anna Marie says, adjusting the tab so it at least lies flat against her shoe.

"Oh, but don't worry. Your real present is coming later."

"Oh. Um. Okay, well, thank you again. . . ." Anna Marie, speechless, twice in one night? She shrugs at us and pops the top on her own soda can, leaving her tab in place. "Let's start. Who wants to go first?"

"I will," Paige says, surprising exactly no one. Paige loves being the center of attention. She gives an evil wiggle of her eyebrows and then says, "I never . . . have been swimming at night."

No one touches the bowl of M&M's.

Paige wrinkles her nose and then turns to Anna Marie. "Your turn."

Anna Marie takes an extra-slow sip of her soda and seems like she's deep in thought. I can tell Paige is about 2.2 seconds away from getting on Anna Marie's case, when Anna Marie finally takes a deep breath and says, "Okay, let's see. Omigosh, this is hard. You know how when you need to think of something and your mind goes completely blank? That's totally happening to me right now—no, wait! I got one! I never faked being sick to miss school."

Paige pops candy into her mouth, while I laugh and sit on my hands. "My mom would see *right* through that. Half the time school is more fun than my house anyway. At least there I can wear lip gloss in peace."

"I don't need to fake sick to stay home," Veronica says. "I'm homeschooled, so I'm already *there*. Sometimes I fake sick so I can go to the doctor, though. I love getting shots."

No one knows how to respond to this, so there's silence for a moment until Veronica cheerfully says, "My turn next! I never read the last page first on a new volume of *Get Fuzzy*."

Surprise, surprise, no one reaches for the bowl. Veronica stares at the rest of us. "Wow, you guys are disciplined too."

Paige just moves on. "Meghan, you're up."

I know *exactly* what to say now that it's my turn. I look right at Paige and give her my most innocent grin when I say, "I never . . . kissed a boy." I've been dying to know the answer to this one ever since Paige got back from summer camp and started acting all mysterious whenever the topic of kissing came up.

Paige tilts her head and raises her eyebrows at me. "I'm impressed, Megs. Way to kick it up a notch."

She looks each of us in the face, waiting to see if anyone will reach for a chocolate. Then she very slowly slips her hand into the bowl and extracts one green M&M, smiling as she pops it into her mouth.

"Omigosh, *Paige*! Who? Was it that guy from camp last summer? And why didn't you *tell* us?" Anna Marie jumps up and pretends to throttle Paige, but in the struggle, Veronica's Mountain Dew gets knocked over, causing us all to scream so loudly, we barely hear the doorbell ringing above our heads.

Anna Marie holds up her hand to shush us and then whispers, "Who the heck could that be?"

Veronica wipes her glasses clean on her shirt. "Oh. That's probably my present."

CHAPTER FOUR

Imagine Your Happy Place

We race up the steps, giggling and tripping, but right as we reach the top, we hear Anna Marie's little brother open the door.

"Who are *you*?" Max asks. Paige opens the basement door a crack, and all four of us peek out at the front entrance. We have to squeeze along the top two steps so our heads line up one on top of the other in order for us all to see.

"Call me Madame Mesmer," says this wispy, otherworldly voice. I can't see the person talking because she's still outside. "I'm the hypnotist, here for the birthday party show."

Hypnotist? I can't turn my head to look at my friends because of the way we're wedged in, but I hear Paige whisper, "Cooooool."

Max tugs his friend into the doorway next to him. "Hypnotist? That's so great. Are you gonna hypnotize my sister? Can you get her to be my slave? Dude, how killer would that be?"

"Hypnotism doesn't work like that, my child," Madame Mesmer says. "But if you don't invite me in, I might just work my magic on you so you will hiccup from now until next week."

Max looks nervous. "Oh, um, no, thanks. I hate hiccups. Please. Please come right in!"

A woman steps into the hallway, and now I can see the person who matches the voice. She's extra-tall and skinny, wearing clunky Mary Jane heels and swaying a little bit in this super-long, filmy skirt. It's impossible to see what color her hair is since she has it all hidden underneath a velvet turban that's wrapped tightly around her head. But her eyebrows are thick and dark and her lips are painted a deep maroon. She has these two spots on her cheeks that look like blush, but if so, she needs the tutorial Paige's sister gave us on blending. As she shakes off her bright-orange coat, the dozens of bangles marching up her arms clang against each other in a weirdly musical way. She looks a little like she bought a Halloween costume marked GYPSY at Party Central. Someone elbows me, but somehow we all manage to hold in our giggles. Right below me, Veronica softly breathes an "oooohhhh."

Madame Mesmer glances around the entryway and then says, "I presume your sister is the birthday girl. Where would I find her? And what about your parents?"

"My mom is taking a bath, and I have instructions only to

interrupt her in case of an emergency. Think this counts as one?"

"I'd venture not," Madame Mesmer says, adjusting her turban with both hands. Each of her fingers has a clunky ring on them. As if she senses our presence or something, she turns toward the basement door.

Veronica gasps and loses her balance. She tumbles forward into the hallway, taking the rest of us down with her like we're a bunch of bowling pins. All four of us sprawl across the wood floor.

"Um, hi," Anna Marie offers from her spot on the ground.

The woman seems completely unconcerned that four kids have basically fallen at her feet. "Hello. I'm Madame Mesmer."

Paige grins and pops up. "Score one for Veronica. This is *actually* a Grade A present. Follow us."

I get up way more slowly, brushing off my butt and trying to get out of Madame Mesmer's way. The funny gut-churning feeling from when we were looking at horror movie titles is back. I don't know anything about hypnosis.

Paige leads the way while the hypnotist glides behind. Max and his friend try to sneak down the steps after us, but Anna Marie notices right away and says, "Oh no. Not you, doofuses!" and points them back to the first floor. They groan and moan pretty loudly about it, but eventually they slam the door.

Veronica immediately begins picking things up from around the room (the bowl of M&M's, her stack of *Get Fuzzy* comics, the cans of soda we'd abandoned when our game of I Never got interrupted) and stacking them on the wood bar. "I don't know how much space you'll need," she says to the strange woman.

"Are you Veronica?" Madame Mesmer asks, referring to a sheet of paper in her hand.

"Yup, that's me. And that's Anna Marie—it's her thirteenth birthday tomorrow."

"Hi," says Anna Marie again, with a tiny wave. Madame Mesmer gives her a cool smile in return. She is a lot bit creepy, and I can tell by the expression on Anna Marie's face that my best friend feels the same way. Paige, of course, seems nothing but calm and collected. As usual. Ugh. How do some people get so lucky not to be scared of anything? I feel like I'm nervous about ev-ery-thing.

Madame Mesmer arches one eyebrow and launches into this long spiel:

"Welcome, girls. I am Madame Mesmer, queen of hypnosis. I will help you explore the hidden depths of your subconscious. If you're open to my talents, you will experience a show of epic proportions, where you'll expand your mind and challenge your preconceptions."

I avoid the other girls' eyes. I get that this is a party act, but at the same time, it feels like something is tickling its way up my spine and into the pit of my stomach, where it flies around like a bee trapped underneath a drinking glass. I'm so not used to this weird combination of fear and excitement that comes with trying something completely unknown. I sneak a peek at Madame Mesmer's turban and clunky rings and decide, yes, this definitely has the potential to be epic. The question is: epic good or epic *bad*?

"Please be seated," the hypnotist orders. We all follow her instruction obediently, arranging ourselves in a semicircle on the floor, the sectional couch propping up our backs. Everyone else seems intent on avoiding eye contact with Madame Mesmer, but I steal glances at her from underneath my lashes. I totally suspect Paige is trying not to burst out laughing (if Paige isn't afraid of anything, she's not gonna start now with a woman who mixes orange and yellow in her outfit), but Anna Marie looks superserious, and Veronica is leaning forward breathlessly.

"Very good." Madame Mesmer nods, her eyes settling eerily on each of us. When she stares me down, it's all I can do not to shiver. Eventually, she moves on. Creeeeeepy.

"Now, let's cover a few basics before I begin. Hypnosis is an ancient and powerful art, and you will explore it under my trained tutelage. If you open your mind to the suggestion of what we're doing here tonight, you will find it easier to enter into the trancelike state that is called hypnosis. Contrary to popular belief, you will not be asleep. You will experience something more akin to a daydream. You will be in full control of your body at all times and very aware of your actions. I can't make you do anything you don't want to do."

Anna Marie giggles, which I can tell is out of nervousness, and Paige shoots her a look that very clearly says, *Zip it!* Madame Mesmer watches us all quietly before continuing.

"You will feel very relaxed, and you will lose all inhibitions. You will be steered by your subconscious, the part of you that controls your actions in the background so subtly, you aren't aware of it. For example, when you breathe in and out, you aren't aware of every breath. That action is controlled by your subconscious. But under hypnosis, your subconscious will drive your actions. You won't feel the need to weigh and measure every act. You will just go with everything."

This time Veronica giggles. (I don't know her well enough to tell if it's nerves or not and, considering how many other times tonight she's said the exact opposite of what I thought she would, I can't even begin to guess how she's feeling about any of this. Except it was her idea. Maybe she's even done this before.) Anna Marie elbows her and says, "Shh." As if she hadn't been doing the exact same thing moments before. But I'm not about to turn on my best friend.

On the one hand, I really wish I could switch off the part of my brain that makes me so cautious about everything. How great would it be to just go with the flow? But on the other hand, I don't know if my brain will let me do it, even if I want to. I also don't know if I trust Madame Mesmer. Or hypnosis.

I trust *me*. I may be cautious, but at least that's gotten me all the way to twelve and three-quarters in one piece. Tonight was supposed to be all about trying out a whole new, fun Meghan, but this feels like a little too much, a little too fast. I want to let go on my own terms, after weighing the danger factors and all the other stuff I might need to consider.

Um, I think I might be really, really bad at being Fun Meghan. Sigh.

Madame Mesmer continues. "If I suggest something silly that you might not do under normal circumstances—such as braying like a donkey, for instance—you will be happy to do it because you won't feel self-conscious in the least. You'll just find it fun. Does that make sense?"

All four of us nod, but then Veronica raises her hand like she's in school. Madame Mesmer points to her. "Yes?"

"Well, I just wondered. What if we normally wouldn't feel self-conscious about braying like a donkey in front of people?"

For a second it looks like Madame Mesmer wants to smile, but then the single eyebrow goes up again and she simply says, "In that case, we'll have to find something else for you to do."

She claps her hands, and I jump a little. I wasn't expecting that. My stomach burns with either nerves or pizza gas (but I'm guessing nerves), even though everything Madame Mesmer is saying sounds really okay, and maybe even fun. *It's just fear of the unknown,* I tell myself. It doesn't exactly calm me down.

"Shall we get started?" Madame Mesmer asks.

All four of us nod, and I hope no one notices my nod isn't exactly enthusiastic.

"Okay, then. I want everyone to silence all cell phones or anything else that could provide a distraction."

Paige and Anna Marie fiddle with their phones. I'd turned off my Ladybug phone the instant I got into the car with Paige. The thing was nothing but sheer embarrassment, and the less I had to acknowledge it, the better. One phone call to my mom before bed, and then I can ignore the phone again until pickup time tomorrow afternoon. Veronica must not have a phone, because she just sits there, smiling at all of us.

Madame Mesmer flicks off some lights and drapes a few scarves she's brought across the rest of the lamps so that the room is cast in this weird, sort of spooky glow. "Make your-selves as comfortable as possible," she says. "Feel free to lie down if you'd like."

We all obey. It seems like she wants us to, even if she phrased it as a suggestion. I hug my legs to my chest for just a second or two and give myself a tiny pep talk that mostly includes the words, *Breathe. Just breathe.* I remind myself that we're in Anna Marie's basement. Mrs. Guerrero is right upstairs, tak-ing a bath. When this part of the party is over, we'll probably just paint our toenails and watch TV until it's time to climb into our sleeping bags (or cot, if you're Veronica) and whisper secrets about which movie star we're crushing on (hello, Graham Cabot all the way) and what three items we'd want if we were stranded on a desert island. I already have mine picked out: my iPod, with one of those solar batteries that recharges in the sunlight; an array of shovels so I can spend my days making incredible sand sculptures and also SOS sand letters that planes could see from the sky; and a fishing net . . . because, entertainment aside, a girl's gotta eat.

"All right. Close your eyes, please," Madame Mesmer says in a voice just above a whisper. "Now I'd like you to imagine yourself in your happy place, somewhere that is relaxing to you. It might be the beach. It might be a field of grass. Wherever you are, take a moment to look around. Now feel your surroundings. Feel the sun on your face and the sand or the grass under your feet."

I wiggle my toes but keep my eyes screwed shut. I try extra-hard to picture the art room at school with my class's latest still-life paintings hanging to dry and the pottery wheel in the back corner. It's fuzzy, but I force my brain to stay there. Is this working?

"Good," says Madame Mesmer. Her skirt swishes and her bangles clatter as she weaves her way among us, stepping over our legs. "Working bottom to top, you're going to let each part of your body relax. Relax your ankles. Now press the backs of your knees into the floor. Feel them getting heavy and connecting with the carpet. Next relax your bum."

I can't believe none of us giggle over the word *bum*. I have one about to bubble out of my throat, but I stop it with an exhale, letting my (mostly flat—blergh) chest rise and fall with deep breaths. This whole time my eyelids have been fluttering because they want so badly to peek, but now they finally relax, and I start to concentrate only on Madame Messmer's voice. It's soooo soothing. Maybe I *can* do this. Maybe I *can* let go.

"Next I want you to imagine yourself flying through the air. Swoop your arms low on one side; now dip to the other. The wind is in your hair; you are a bird, incapable of falling. Just feel the freedom of flight; let the joy of it bubble up in your chest. Take a rest on a puffy cloud and then swoosh back through the air again."

The room is totally silent, except for Madame Mesmer's voice. Is anything happening? I don't *feel* anything happening. But I'm going with it. I think maybe I even *want* it to work.

"Okay, now, when I count to ten, I want you to slip into a deep state of hypnosis. One . . . two . . . three . . ." She continues to count until she reaches, "Nine . . . ten. You are now in a state of hypnosis. You are safe. Your entire body feels relaxed and free. You are peaceful as you sink into a deeper and deeper state of hypnosis. You are safe. You are free."

PART TWO

PART TWO

CHAPTER FIVE

One-a-Chick, Two-a-Chick

Take me to New York. I'd like to see LA. I really want to come kick it with you. You'll be my American boy. . . .

I bolt upright, tangling my legs in my sleeping bag.

"What the what?"

The music from Summer Dance Party blares from the TV so loudly, I think the police might show up. There's something hard underneath my butt; I scoot over, yank the remote out from my jumbled mess of covers, and jam my finger on the power button.

Ahhhhh. Blissful quiet.

Without the glare from the flat-screen, the room also goes to mostly dark, but there's some crack-of-dawn light streaming in from the half windows, enough so I can make out the shapes of my friends as they start to stir. I can't imagine how any of them slept through *that*.

A beam of light shines directly into my eyes, forcing me to throw a hand over my face. "Paige! Seriously?"

"This flashlight app comes in handy," Paige replies.

I respond by bunching up a sweatshirt I find next to me and chucking it at Paige. Too bad I miss by a mile.

On the cot in the corner, Veronica says, "Christmas is crunchy," then lies back down and promptly resumes snoring. Loudly.

I sure hope I don't talk in my sleep. Or snore. I've never been able to ask anyone before because I'm always sleeping alone in my room and there hasn't been anyone *to* ask. But it suddenly hits me that I'm here. It's the next day, and I'm here! My brain is still early morning fuzzy, so I don't really remember making the conscious decision to stay last night, but clearly I must have. I hug my covers around me and celebrate with a happy little shoulder jiggle. I did it! My first true sleepover.

Paige plops back down and snuggles into her sleeping bag again, but from the way she's huffing and puffing and sighing all annoyedlike, I'm guessing she isn't going to be able to get back to sleep. And knowing Paige, her philosophy will be: If *she's* up, then the whole world should be too.

Might as well beat her to it.

I unzip my bag and use my legs to push the cover the rest of the way off. Then I stand. My eyes are still adjusting and the sun isn't bright enough through the windows yet, so all

I can make out are dark shapes. I know the basement pretty well, but we pushed a lot of furniture around last night. Plus there are people sleeping in places we usually walk. Nothing seems familiar, and I don't trust myself not to trip on something or some*one*, so I drop to my knees and crawl toward the wall, feeling pretty ridiculous.

Halfway there something brushes against my face, and I very nearly scream. My hand swipes at my cheek, and I catch something wispy in my fingers. *Please don't be a spider web, please don't be a spider web. If you have to be a spider web, please, please don't be a spider web with an actual spider attached to you.*

Whatever's in my hand is thin, like spaghetti, slightly sticky, and almost a little spongy-feeling. I bring it close to my face and squint.

Silly String? My brain catalogues the texture between my fingers and confirms the match. Weird. I don't remember any Silly String battles last night. My crawl gets ten times more awkward as I attempt to make forward progress on my hands and knees while also keeping one arm up to sweep the air in front of me for any other unwelcome surprises. When I finally reach the wall, I slide along its length until I'm on my feet at the edge of the room. I stretch my hand along the wall and feel the edge of the flat-screen. That means if I go in the opposite direction I should hit the bank of light switches right about . . . here.

I fumble with the switch in the dark and then flip it on, saying a silent *sorry* to Veronica, who is still snoring.

My jaw drops to the floor right alongside my stomach.

Um, this is all seriously . . . like, whoa. To put it mildly. For starters, there is Silly String ev-ery-where. Wound around the base of the potted plant, looped along the Irish pub signs, threaded through the holes in the net of the Ping-Pong table, and crisscrossing Veronica's body on her cot.

The second the light goes on, and Paige settles the sweatshirt I'd lobbed at her over her face. "Whyisthelighton?" she groans.

"Um, Paige. I think you need to see this."

"Umph," comes through the sweatshirt.

"Seriously, Paige. I *really* think you need to see this." I tiptoe my way through hundreds of Doritos crumbs and popcorn kernels covering the carpet in the corner by the stairs and bend to examine a wrapper covered in sticky melted icecream sandwich remnants. I place it gently in the center of the coffee table, next to a towering pyramid built out of Mountain Dew cans, and wipe my sticky hands on my pajama pants.

Wow. Just . . . wow.

I reach Paige and jostle her shoulder. She still has the sweatshirt over her eyes and an arm draped across that, holding it in place. "C'mon, Paige. Wake. Up. Now!"

She swats at me from under the covers, but I catch her

wrist and tug, dragging her out of the sleeping bag. The sweatshirt falls aside, and I stare into her face.

Paige looks back, opens her mouth . . . and screams.

Which wakes Veronica. And makes *me* scream.

"Eeeeeeeeeep!" we all shriek.

"What's happening?" My voice is high-pitched, like I've inhaled helium. I turn to Veronica—wait, is she wearing footie pajamas? No time to think about that right this second— who blinks at me once before her mouth drops open. Oh God. I get a bad taste in my mouth that doesn't have anything to do with morning breath. Why are they looking at me like I grew a second nose overnight? My hands fly to my face, and I dart frantic looks back and forth between the two of them. Why aren't they saying anything?

"What? What is it? Do I have a giant zit, because that happens sometimes and I can't—"

"It's not that." Paige's forehead goes all crinkly. "It's . . . Oh man, I don't know how to . . ."

"You're missing an eyebrow," Veronica blurts.

Say *what*?

My fingertips move from my cheeks to my eyes, and I begin feeling above them. I brush distinctive fuzz, and there's a reassuring, soft scritching sound as I explore the ridge above my right eye. But then I move my fingers to the same spot above my left eye and . . . it's disturbingly smooth, like the skin of an apple.

No. No, no, no, no, no, *no*!

This cannot be happening.

I kick aside a pillow and step over Paige in a race to the bathroom, not even stopping to get grossed out over something gooey I step in. I grab the door handle and push down, but it doesn't budge. I jiggle it a few times and am just lifting my fist to pound when it opens inward, throwing me off-balance.

Max, in plaid flannel pajama bottoms and a matching top, blinks at me; then, after a beat or two, grins. "Classic," he says, laughing as he slides past me.

Ugh! I feel like screaming again, but I bite it back and slam the door shut behind me. Then I creep to the sink, prop my hands on the sides, and lean in close to the mirror.

Oh. Heavenly. Heckweasels!

I have one eyebrow. ONE! I stare and stare, but no amount of blinking shows me anything different than a one-eyebrowed freak. This cannot be happening. Can. Not. My life is ruined. It takes a few moments of gaping into the mirror for my brain to start moving again and, when it does, it's completely full of questions I have zip—zero—answers for.

At the top of the list: how long does it take for eyebrows to grow, anyway? Surely, longer than a few hours, which is all I have before my mom comes to pick me up and take me to handbell practice at church. Could a hat hide it? Makeup?

I mean, obviously I'm not allowed to wear makeup, but maybe Paige can work some magic so my parents won't notice.

Oh God, but then there's school! There is *no way* I can go to school on Monday with one eyebrow—and it's not like I'll have Paige at my house in the morning to help even if she *could* find a way to hide it with makeup. Plus our school has a no-hats-indoors policy, so that won't work.

"Megs?" Paige taps gently on the other side of the door. "Are you okay? Can I do anything?"

"I'm fine. I just need to . . . process."

I go back to thinking as hard as I can.

A headband? I've seen some high school girls wearing a thin ribbon around their foreheads in some hippie-bohemian kind of look. Would anyone buy it if I suddenly went boho?

No. Of course they wouldn't.

Could I get a fake eyebrow? Some kind of stick-on one like the mustache I wore last Halloween when I went to the party at school dressed as Luigi from Super Mario Bros.? Or maybe like the toupee our mailman wears, which I always try so hard not to stare at whenever he hands me the stack of catalogs and bills for my parents?

Let's face it. My life is over. *O-v-e-r.*

I don't even want to *think* of the nickname I'll probably end up with after this. What if it follows me to college? What if I want to run for president one day, and all the people I knew in middle school resurface to tell the whole world about the time I had a unibrow, and not from lack of tweezing above my nose? Or what if I *still have it*? What if it *NEVER* grows back?

For a long time all I can do is stare into the mirror, not really seeing the reflection but working through and shooting down forty-seven million more harebrained schemes to possibly save me from my mother's screeching and, more important, from the bottom rungs of the social ladder at school. But then a small movement in the mirror, just behind my reflected shoulder, catches my eye.

What on earth . . . ?

I spin to face the bathtub and am greeted by a slew of tiny, fluffy balls on legs. I slump back against the sink and begin counting. One. Two, Three. Four. Five, Six . . . There are sixteen baby chicks happily parading around the empty bathtub! But *why* are there sixteen baby chicks parading around the bathtub? Why am I missing an eyebrow? What did I step in on the way to the bathroom, and why are there Silly String loops connecting the faucet to the shower nozzle? What is even happening right now?

I pause. There's something else that isn't quite adding up. Well, obviously, there is way, *way* more about this morning that isn't adding up, but there's something big I'm missing. It's pushing its way into my brain except I can't quite grasp it.

And then I do.

I yank open the bathroom door.

I ignore Paige and Veronica, who are staring at me in pity, and march straight to Paige's sleeping bag where I reach in and grab the sweatshirt that had been right next to me when I woke up this morning. The one I'd thrown at Paige when she aimed the flashlight app at my face. I hold it up and gulp. The air in the basement chokes me, and there's a slight tilt to the room.

"Whoa," says Paige in an awestruck voice. "Is that . . . ?"

"Jake Ribano's sweatshirt," I say breathlessly, with a combination of wonder and fear. This is big. This is, quite possibly, bigger than a trashed basement. Bigger than a flock of chicks in the bathtub. Maybe, *maybe*, even bigger than a missing eyebrow.

Jake Ribano is never, ever, *ever* seen without his trademark black sweatshirt with the giant white skull and crossbones across the front. It lets all the kids know Jake Ribano is Trouble with a capital *T*.

And now I'm holding it? *The* sweatshirt!

I have to figure all this out. I watched a movie once where everyone woke up in an alternate universe and had to find their way back. Maybe that's it! If I could just quiet the buzzing in my brain . . . *You're smart. You can make sense out of this, Meghan.*

"Wow. Who do you guys think this belongs to?" Paige is holding up this weird, superfuzzy, supertall hat that looks like someone wrapped it in a carpet remnant. It has a maroon ribbon along the bottom and a hideous tassel on the top part. Paige plops it onto her head, and it wobbles there until she slides the chin strap on. "Is this the best, or what? Next year's Halloween costume, ya think?"

"Where did that come from?" I ask.

Paige shrugs. "Dunno. It was right at the end of my sleeping bag."

"Um, guys?" Veronica's voice is nasally and grating and cuts through the quiet I'm trying to find. I so badly want to be nice for my best friend's sake, but I seriously wonder how anyone could expect me to process what is happening *and* deal with Veronica politely.

Paige is clearly not concerned with being sweet. "Not now, Veronica."

Veronica sniffles once and then says in a tiny voice, "But, um, this is kinda important."

I stare numbly at the sweatshirt I have clenched in my fist and try to tune out their exchange. *Think, Meghan, think.*

"What?" Paige snaps.

Veronica makes a harrumph sound and turns her back on

us. She bends over her cot and begins letting the air out of her mattress. "Forget it then! I just thought you might also be noticing, or I guess the word would be more like *wondering*. . . . I mean—"

"Spit it out!" Paige orders, and I cringe. Veronica falls onto the half-filled mattress, which hisses air angrily.

"Well, it's just . . . ," she says, her arms spreading wide to take in the whole room. "Where is Anna Marie?"

CHAPTER SIX

Ninja Nancy Drews

I let my eyes rest on the empty sleeping bag I could have sworn had been filled with my best friend's warm body at bedtime last night. Or this morning. I can't actually remember what time we finally went to bed, but it had most definitely, positively been in the a.m. hours. Come to think of it, though, I can't be totally sure, because I can't remember much of last night.

I've been trying so hard to clear my head so I can figure this all out, but why hadn't I started with the basics? Like *what really happened* last night? I remember Madame Mesmer telling me to lie down on the floor, and each of us staking out a space on the rug to follow her directions. I remember breathing deeply and trying not to laugh when she told us to relax our bums, but after that . . . ? Nothing. I can almost believe I'd just fallen asleep for the night then and there, but if so—how can we explain any of *this*?

I look around the room again. Everywhere my eyes rest, I see disaster. The tower of Mountain Dew cans on the coffee table reaches far above my head like a giant game of Jenga. The ceiling fan spins a long, slow trail of Silly String around and around, around and around. The floor is covered in Doritos crumbs, popped popcorn kernels, and the spilled contents of an entire bowl of M&M's, just waiting to be ground into the thick carpet.

There is no way I could have slept through all *this* mess being made. *No. Possible. Way.* And yet I don't remember even one second of the night in which this kind of disaster zone could have been created. I take a tentative step onto my sleeping bag to avoid the booby-trapped carpet of stains-waiting-to-happen.

"Take me to New York. I'd like to see LA. I really want to . . ."

I drop to the ground, frantically tossing my sleeping bag until I uncover the remote. I jam my finger on the off button again and again.

Quiet.

I crouch and take a deep breath. Veronica and Paige are frozen in place, clearly having the exact same thoughts, and the three of us stare at one another before I finally whisper, "What's happening, you guys?"

Almost as if my words snap her out of a trance, Veronica flings a leg over the back of the sofa and kind of half climbs, half rolls onto the cushions and down to the floor, landing between me and Paige. She brushes her hands off, shrugs at us, and then crawls over to Anna Marie's sleeping bag and puts her hand inside, patting around.

"She's obviously not hiding in there, Veronica. She's small, but she's not that small," Paige says, clearly biting back a sigh.

"Clue number one! It's cold!" Veronica proclaims.

"Huh?" I ask.

"This sleeping bag is cold. No one's been inside here for a long time. Maybe even hours." Veronica sounds pretty sure of herself, even under the weight of Paige's squinty stare.

"She probably got uncomfortable on the floor and remembered she has a comfy, cozy bed right upstairs. So let's go find her!" Paige, who is always confident, sounds even more sure of herself than normal, and right away I realize, *of course*, that has to be exactly what happened. It's beyond logical. A swarm of insects with wings had taken up residence in my belly the second Veronica made the comment about Anna Marie being missing, but now they die out, as though an exterminator showed up inside my stomach. Anna Marie is fine. One problem solved. Maybe the mystery of the basement mess will be just as obvious once we're all back together again and can piece together what happened after Madame Mesmer left last night.

Paige stands and holds out a hand to help me up. Once

on my feet, I take a step toward Paige, then stop, reach back down, and grab Jake's sweatshirt. I slip it on and zip it over my hot pink KEEP CALM AND BAKE CUPCAKES T-shirt. It's just . . . I have the thing now, so I might as well wear it while I—oh wow—it smells like boy too. The good kind of soap-and-mint boy smell, not the sweaty-socks-and-soccer-practice kind of boy smell.

"Wha-*at?*" I ask, all fake innocence, when I notice Paige's raised eyebrows. Then I moan because I can't do raised eye-brows*ssss* anymore. Just raised eye*brow*. Singular. I slap a hand above my eye and rub at the ridge of smooth skin again. Somehow with all the bigger mysteries of the last few minutes, I'd managed to forget, but now all I can picture is my image in the bathroom mirror. My mother is going to have a complete and total conniption. She won't even let me try *bangs* because she feels strongly that long layers suit my face shape better. She'll never, ever let me spend the night out of the house again. And I was *just* getting good at it. Sort of. I didn't freak out and demand to go home at bedtime, but I'm not sure it counts if I can't actually remember lights-out.

If I want any prayer at all of ever being allowed to leave the house again, we need to move fast. Step one: wake up Anna Marie pronto and get her down here. Step two: find a way to get this place cleaned up before Anna Marie's mom sees it, because if she does . . . disaster. I mean, she's usually pretty chill and it *is* a sleepover, so I'm mostly sure she expected some regular party mess. But *this*? A piece of Silly String detaches from the fan and lands on my arm. This goes way beyond. And if Mrs. Guerrero mentions anything about any of it to my mom, I'm doubly dead. As in, my mom will kill me and then find a way to bring me back from the dead just so she can kill me again.

Paige tugs on my sleeve, and we tiptoe carefully through the minefield of spilled food. Operation Wake Up Anna Marie is on. We're almost to the stairs when Veronica races up behind us, huffing like she's just run a race, despite the fact that the distance between the sleeping bags and the stairs is about ten steps, fifteen at most. She grabs my sweatshirt at the elbow, bunching the fabric between her hand. "Wait!"

We pause. I'm getting used to Veronica's weird behavior now, and so I wait patiently, not even bothering to exchange secret smirking glances with Paige. Veronica puts her free hand up in a crossing guard's stop motion. "We definitely can't let her mom see us," she says.

"Why not?" I ask. As long as the encounter isn't taking place down here, what's the harm?

"Be-caaaaaause. If Anna Marie *isn't* up there, then her mom is going to have all kinds of questions for us. And she's probably going to ask them *after* she's stormed down to this basement to make sure Anna Marie's not here. Do we really want Mrs. Guerrero to see all this?" She releases my sweatshirt to gesture around the room. First I have to stretch Jake's sweatshirt carefully back into place, smoothing down the wrinkles Veronica's fist caused. But then my eyes fall on a pizza box I hadn't noticed before. A fly is crawling on one of the half-eaten pieces. And wait, is that a giant blob of Cool Ranch dip on the corner of the couch? Ugh.

Of *course* Anna Marie is up there. Where else would she be? But letting Mrs. Guerrero know we're awake might make her want to come downstairs to help us pack up or something. That could not, repeat *not*, happen. "She has a point," I say.

"Veronica, I have to give you credit. You're totally right," Paige adds.

Veronica blushes and sticks out her chest a little. "I completed the Junior Hardy Boys Detective Certification Course."

Um, oooooookayyyyyyy.

"Well, since I don't know how to respond to that, I'm just going to move on," Paige says, gripping the banister. "Okay, so let's be superquiet, girls. Stick together and *do not make a noise.*"

"I also take ninja lessons," Veronica whispers when we reach the top stair.

Paige goes first, easing the basement door open and motioning with hand signals for me to follow. Then she waves on

Veronica, and soon all three of us are pressed against the hallway wall, ears straining hard for any noises that will clue us in to everyone's whereabouts. In the kitchen a television is reporting on an Upstate New York teen who forgot his keys and got stuck in his chimney while attempting to get into his house. There's the sound of silverware clanging against a plate.

I stare hard at the yellow-and-white flowered wallpaper in the hallway until all the petals blur, and I try to quiet my heartbeat. Paige swings her head in the opposite direction from the kitchen and slides along the wall toward the stairs to the upper level. She gestures for us to follow. Tiptoeing, we take the carpeted stairs one at a time, pausing every so often to listen for approaching footsteps. I barely breathe until we've squeezed through the door into Anna Marie's room.

Even before I spy the perfectly made canopy bed with its white eyelet comforter and the giant purple-and-green peace sign pillow that Anna Marie and I sewed from felt last Christmas vacation, I can tell the room is empty. It just *feels* empty. Paige, Veronica, and I exchange quick looks but barely have time to process anything before we hear someone climbing the stairs.

"Hide!" I whisper-yell. I dive onto the ground, rolling under Anna Marie's bed, and brush the pleated bed skirt aside to peek out from underneath. Paige slides smoothly into the closet, and I watch her nudge aside a jumble of clothes and shoes before noiselessly closing the door. Veronica spins in a circle a few times before plopping heavily into the corner of the bedroom where a bunch of stuffed animals are perfectly arranged. It's a good thing Anna Marie isn't here because she might just kill Veronica for that. I feel relatively safe under Anna Marie's bed as I watch Veronica try to blend in among a zoo's worth of creatures, propping the stuffed giraffe on her arm and a parrot that was a souvenir from a trip to Key West on her shoulder. She finishes by dropping a floppy dog (who I happen to know is named Newbury and who is Anna Marie's favorite) on her head. Veronica might as well be wearing a flashing look-at-me sign, but she sits 200 percent as still as the animals, in her one-piece footed pajamas, seemingly convinced she is completely camouflaged.

I'm seriously in awe of how long the girl can go without blinking. It's, like, superhuman. I get so absorbed in trying to match her (not possible—the more I think about not blinking, the more I positively *have to* blink), I barely register that the sound of whatever tune Mrs. Guerrero had been humming as she'd climbed the steps is fading.

I let out my breath in a whoosh (and also blink a whole bunch).

But after a few more seconds the humming grows louder again and stops right outside Anna Marie's door. My heart pounds in my ears. *Why* did we hide in the first place? Mrs. Guerrero knows we're in the house. Why didn't we just let ourselves get discovered in Anna Marie's room and then make up some excuse about finding something Anna Marie wanted us to bring downstairs? If Mrs. Guerrero comes in and spots Veronica pretending to be a stuffed panda and then I roll out from under the bed and Paige pops out of the closet, what are we even supposed to say? Operation Wake Up Anna Marie is the worst-planned, worst-executed operation in the history of forever.

But as I lie here, desperately trying to come up with any excuse that doesn't sound totally lame, the footsteps move down the hall, and there's a light rapping on a door. Not Anna Marie's door, thank the gods.

Mrs. Guerrero's voice is muffled, but I can just make out some of the words. "Outside . . . weed garden . . . rain later. Leave the . . . alone. I suspect they were up late and . . . sleep in. Okay?"

Max must answer something because the footsteps turn and head back down the stairs.

The coast is clear.

Phew!

Paige slips out of the closet and does nothing more than shake her head at Veronica as Anna Marie's future stepsister untangles herself from the slew of stuffed animals. Once I'm on my feet, the three of us creak open the door and peer into the hallway. All quiet.

Max's door is closed, and there's muffled talking inside. I creep over and press my ear against it, listening hard. *Boys*, I mouth. Definitely not Anna Marie's slightly pip-squeaky voice talking to her baby brother. More likely whatever friend Max had over last night is still here. Or back. It doesn't matter, really. All that matters is, it isn't my best friend in there. My shoulders droop.

We work our way along the hall, taking inchy-squinchy steps and peeking into the rooms. An empty bathroom, an empty guest room, and Mrs. Guerrero's empty bedroom. No Anna Marie.

I follow Paige slowly down the stairs, hugging the wall with my back like a real spy as we pass through the dining room and then the living room, which is totally neat and clean for the company they're having later, but it's completely empty.

The TV is still on in the kitchen, and the announcer's voice from the worst car dealership ad ever (that also happens to come on during every other commercial break) covers the sound of Paige creeping up to the doorway. Veronica hums right along with the "From sedans to Winnebagos to SUVs, we've got the wheels to make you groovy" jingle. Paige slaps a hand over Veronica's mouth.

"Shhhhhh!" Paige hisses.

Veronica shrugs. She may be kind of weird, but I gotta sympathize with her. Even if the jingle is totally awful and doesn't even really rhyme, it *is* hard not to sing along.

Paige steps into the doorway, slowly drops her hand, and squints as she listens. When the TV quiets for a second between a commercial and the start of the news (one big hint it's not Anna Marie in there), I can hear the clink-clink of a spoon stirring against a mug. Hint number two: Anna Marie does not drink coffee. Paige holds up her hand to signal absolute quiet, but after a few more seconds she shakes her head once. Not a surprise. I already know Anna Marie isn't in there with her mom. If she were, they'd be talking to each other. Anna Marie can barely stop chattering long enough to brush her teeth.

Just to make absolute sure, we wait another long minute, during which Paige and I try desperately to block out the sight of Veronica practicing her ninja moves in the empty living room. The seconds tick on as Mrs. Guerrero rinses a dish, turns on the dishwasher, and then opens the refrigerator and closes it again. No way would Anna Marie keep silent this long.

She isn't in the kitchen.

She isn't in her bedroom.

She isn't in the house at all.

CHAPTER SEVEN

The Terms of a Pucker-Up

We can breathe regularly once we're back in the basement and plopped on the giant sectional. I pull my legs up to my chest and look helplessly at Paige and Veronica, hoping they'll have some kind of a plan. Too bad they have the same expression I do.

"Let's call her phone," Paige suggests, rummaging through her bag. "Where's *my* phone?"

We help her look and unearth it a moment later in the bottom of the popcorn bowl. She frowns, brushes salt from the glittery silver case, and presses the button to call Anna Marie. "It's ringing!" she says after a second.

At the exact same time, something buzzes near Anna Marie's sleeping bag. We look at each other, and then I crawl over and push aside Anna Marie's pillow. Sure enough, one cell phone, in silent mode, vibrates in my hand. Paige pushes end on the call.

"Now what?" I moan. I'm not trying to be the voice of doom and gloom, but this is so far from the "epic" I had in mind, it isn't even funny. The sinking feeling in my stomach is just about the worst thing ever. Worse than the time I left Hippy in a restaurant booth when we stopped for lunch on a road trip to Indiana, and I had to endure this whole entire lecture from my dad about "acting responsible" when I made him turn around after we'd been back on the highway for an hour. Worse than the time Anna Marie and I fought over whether she should have sent me letters from camp more than twice all summer, given that she knew I wasn't allowed to go to overnight camp (er, given my sleepover mishaps) and could only experience it through Anna Marie's descriptions.

Wow do I really, really, *really* wish Anna Marie were just off at camp right now, instead of . . . wherever she might be. A lump forms in my throat as I picture all the horrible scenarios my mom feels the need to warn me about every time I leave the house on my own. What if something really bad happened to Anna Marie? What if she's hurt somewhere? Or worse?

No. I can't let my brain go there. I turn to Paige. "How are we supposed to tell Mrs. Guerrero we've lost her only daughter? On her *birthday*, no less! My mother is going to send me to boarding school. Or something more horrible. She'll probably shave my other eyebrow and send me to *our* school. Or, what if the FBI comes to ask us questions about Anna Marie since we were the last ones to see her, and that guy from the missing persons show sets up cameras on our lawns and . . . Do you think they'll put Anna Marie's face on a billboard? She hated her school picture this year! She'd die if it were blown up and mounted above the highway."

Okay, so my brain went there.

Paige takes a deep breath. "It's not gonna come to that. Logically speaking, Anna Marie is probably totally fine. We just have to find her before it's time for our parents to pick us up. Your mom's coming at noon, right?"

I nod, miserable right down to the tips of my unpainted toenails. We never did get around to mani-pedis last night. At least I don't think we did. It would be nice if I could remember. I reach down to pull my sock off so I can check for sure. Nope. No pedicure.

Veronica says, "My mom can't pick me up because my brother has his American Coasters Enthusiasts meeting, and they're electing a treasurer today. I'm catching a ride home with Kevin."

"Who's Kevin? Is that your other brother?"

"No, silly. That's Anna Marie's dad. Duh." Veronica rolls her eyes as if we should go around learning and remembering the first names of our friends' parents.

"My mom's coming at noon too," Paige says, ignoring

Veronica's eye roll, which surprises me. "Okay, so it's only"—
Paige hangs off the sofa and tugs her bag closer to her,
grabbing her phone again and swiping it on—"geez. It's not
even seven thirty. On a *weekend*! What are we doing awake?"

Paige is acting like nothing is wrong with our morning
besides the early hour, but I really can't be optimistic right
now. She always assumes everything will work out perfectly
fine, mostly because it always does for her. But I don't want to
just "think good thoughts" and wait for it to be all sunshine
and lollipops. I want my friend in front of me, safe and sound,
and I can't imagine relaxing until that happens. Also? I want
to know everything that happened last night *and* I want to
know *why* I don't know that already.

"Guys?" I ask. "What do you remember from our sleepover?
Because the last thing *I* remember is the hypnotist telling me
to relax and think of my happy place, and I am far, far, *far*
from my happy place right now!"

Paige picks at a loose string on the yoga pants she wore to
bed. "I don't remember anything either," she admits.

Veronica's eyes get wide. "Me either. Do you think Madame
Mesmer put a spell on us?"

Paige snorts. "No, Veronica. I do not think the hypnotist
put a spell on us. She's a party performer, not a witch!"

Veronica shrugs as if Paige's sarcasm doesn't bother her
one tiny bit and continues picking M&M's off the carpet in a

pattern of green, red, brown, green, red, brown, and popping them into her mouth. I scrunch up my nose. I'm hungry too (starved, actually), but . . . ewww. No, thanks.

"I habf an idrea," Veronica says, her mouth full. When this statement is met with blank stares from us, she finishes chewing and tries again. "An idea. I have one. It's Mystery 101, really. We need to start by examining the clues."

"Oh, sorry, right. I forgot you were Harriet the Spy," Paige says, accompanied by an eye roll of her own this time.

"Junior Hardy Boys." Veronica corrects her matter-of-factly, and Paige snorts. I feel bad that Paige isn't at least trying to be nicer to Veronica, but I have to admit, the girl is kind of oblivious to sarcasm. But still. No reason to be rude. I resolve to try even harder because I'm mostly sure Anna Marie would want me to be nice to her future stepsister. What if it were my best friend's dying wish? Wait. No. I *have* to stop thinking like this. We're going to find her in plenty of time, and all will be well. It *has to be*. I live in the suburbs. Horrible things don't happen in the suburbs.

"Veronica's got a point, though," I say, once again forcing my mind to stop wandering to the dark side. "We do need to come up with some sort of plan."

Veronica stands. "Well, for starters, I gotta change out of my gran's diaper."

I know I made a vow mere minutes ago to be kinder toward

Veronica, but really? There is a mathematical probability of zero that I can stop my nose from wrinkling at that. Veronica grabs her backpack and turns toward the bathroom.

Oh my God, oh my God, oh my God. The bathroom! How could I have possibly forgotten?

"Wait!" I call.

Veronica freezes and, next to me on the couch, Paige does the same. I give them both a guilty look. "Okay, you guys are going to think I'm seriously crazy for not mentioning this before now, and I won't blame you," I say, sitting up on my heels. "It's just that, I saw Jake's sweatshirt and I kind of spaced and then we were creeping around upstairs and I— Um, okay, so the thing is . . . there may or may not be sixteen baby chicks in the bathtub."

Paige gapes at me. "Say what now?"

Veronica squeals. "Baby chicks?" She scrambles over the top of the sofa, falls onto the floor, stands and brushes herself off, and then speed walks to the bathroom.

Paige untangles her legs and rises gracefully as ever, following behind. I bring up the rear. All three of us peer into the bathtub at the fuzzy balls of yellow. "Ohhh," whispers Veronica. "They're sooooo cute!"

"They're so cute, but what are they doing *here*?" Paige asks, leaning closer.

And then something else comes back to me.

"Wait, I just remembered. Max! Max was in here this morning when I tried to get in to see my eyebrow. I bet Max knows what they're doing here *and* where Anna Marie is! God, I'm such an idiot for not thinking of that when we were upstairs earlier. I swear, something is happening to my brain today."

"Max," Paige growls. We crash into each other trying to get out of the bathroom at the same time, then half tiptoe, half march across the floor, dodging chips and candy in our effort to get to Anna Marie's bratty brother as fast as we possibly can.

Turns out, we don't have far to go.

The second we reach the stairs, we come face-to-face with Max's video camera.

"Gir-rrrrls," he says in this singsongy voice. "Say something to my fans on YouTube."

"I'm gonna squash you, you brat," Paige says at the same time as I ask, "How long have you been taping us?"

"Long enough," Max answers with a giggle, handing his camera to his little friend. "Lock this in the treasure chest in my room and wait for me," he orders. The friend scrambles up the stairs, and Max turns back to us with his annoying *I may be the devil, and there's nothing you can do about it* grin.

"I'm not kidding, Max. I'm gonna make your life miserable, and not even your sister will be able to protect you. If she'd even want to, which I doubt. Where is she?" Paige asks.

Max's smug smile falls off his face, and his forehead crinkles in confusion. "Where's who?" he asks.

"Your *sister*, you stink breath. And believe me, I'm calling you a million worse names in my head right now."

"What do you mean, where's my sister? She's down here with you. Why wouldn't she be?"

I clasp my fingers around Paige's arm and squeeze. "Is he telling the truth right now?"

Paige squints into Max's face. He blinks, the picture of perfect innocence, and even though I know how fast he can summon that expression whenever Mrs. Guerrero is about to bust him for something, I have to admit it's convincing. Paige speaks very softly and gently. "Are you saying you don't know where your sister is?"

"Are *you* saying you don't know where my sister is?" Max counters.

Veronica pipes up from behind me. "Not a clue. Well, that's not true. We do have clues. There are the chicks in the bathtub, for starters, and the—"

"The chicks!" What is *wrong* with me that I forgot about them *AGAIN*? "Max, you were in the bathroom this morning when I tried to get in. What were you doing down here? Where did those chicks come from?"

Max continues to look confused. "How should I know

where they came from? I was just using the bathroom," he says. "Figured I'd stink up yours instead of mine."

"Gross." Seriously. So gross.

"Come to think of it, I did think they were a little weird." Max shrugs and lifts his eyes to examine the ceiling.

Paige studies him carefully. "Are you telling me you . . . did your business . . . in front of sixteen baby chicks, and you only thought it was *a little weird*?"

"What can I say? I'm a dude." Max shrugs again.

"He has a point there." I may be an only child, but I've met enough boys to say now with perfect certainty, "Boys are total mysteries."

"I'll tell you what's a mystery. A missing person, that's what. Max, are you positive you know nothing?" Paige asks, gripping his arm.

"Oww," Max says, rubbing his elbow once Paige lets go of it. "I don't know where my weirdo sister is. And I'm telling Mom you don't either!" He pushes his butt off the stairs and turns to climb them when all three of us grab on to his legs.

I hold on as tightly as I can to his pajama pants. "Not so fast, Maxamillion!"

"Who's gonna stop me?" Max taunts, but his eyes get extra big when Paige leans in and shakes a fist in his face. He stops struggling and sinks onto the stair. "All right, all right, ladies. No need to resort to violence. I'm sure we can work out a mutually beneficial arrangement."

"A what *what*?" Paige asks.

"I'm just saying. You scratch my back; I'll scratch yours. I won't tell my mom, but it'll cost you."

Paige looks at me and then at Max, clearly smothering a laugh. "Oh yeah, pint-size? What'd you have in mind?"

Max rubs his hands together in glee. "Lemme see now. Meghan, I really like your sweatshirt. We could start there."

"No way, no how." I hug the hoodie around me and fiddle with the zipper. "Besides, it's not mine to bargain with."

"That's the point," Max says, looking momentarily disappointed, but then his eyes light up. "You're a math whiz, though, right? That's all yours to bargain with. You do my homework for a week—no, a month—and I won't breathe a word."

"A month? Are you insane?"

"Fine, three weeks."

I purse my lips, considering. I'm not a cheater, and I can't stand people who are, but, then again, if my parents discover I've lost my best friend (which will happen the minute Max rats us out to his mom), I can kiss my entire social life goodbye for the rest of middle school even if—no, *when*, definitely when—Anna Marie turns up safe and sound. Probably the rest of high school, too. I'll die an old maid, locked away in my room, without even paper lanterns to watch for on my birthday, like that princess in *Tangled*. I cannot accept that.

I have no choice here. At least, not one that makes logical sense when you weigh the pros and cons.

"Two weeks, final offer," I say, and Max grins. He holds out his hand for a shake. Ugh. I swallow a sigh and take his sweaty palm in mine, pumping it once.

"That's settled then," Paige says, brushing her pants off.

"Not so fast. That's just what I want from Meghan. You're next."

Paige's eyebrows (both of them, because she has two, like everyone on this planet with the exception of me) shoot up. Max looks extra-serious as he says, "From you, sweet maiden, I'll take one perfect kiss."

Paige snorts. "Yeah, right." She brushes more invisible lint off her yoga pants.

This time it's Max's turn to raise his eyebrows. (Even bratty Max gets to have two eyebrows. I'm officially weirder than Max, and I didn't even think that was possible.) "Oh, I'm serious. Deadly."

"Why, you little—"

"I'll kiss him," says Veronica, and both Paige and I whirl around to face her.

"What? It's only a peck. I don't care," she says.

Max wrinkles his forehead. "First of all, this is my request of Paige. Second of all, we're gonna be brother and sister in a few weeks, so no way."

Veronica shrugs. "Oh yeah. I forgot about that part. Sorry, Paige. I tried."

Paige studies Max, tilting her head to once side. I hold perfectly still, wondering how my friend is going to respond. I know for a fact, which Paige confirmed last night when we played I Never (side note: Why do I remember that and not much that came after?), that she's only just had her first kiss. Would she really want her second to be with Anna Marie's bratty kid brother? I'm betting no, nope, and he's got a better chance of seeing a unicorn in the wild.

"Here are my conditions," Paige finally says, totally surprising me. "You keep your lips closed at all times, and it lasts no more than three seconds. Four, if you're very lucky."

"Done," agrees Max, fluttering his eyes closed and puckering his lips.

"Not now, dweeb. *After* we find Anna Marie. How else can I be sure you'll keep up your end of the bargain?"

"Well, how can I be sure you will?" Max shoots back.

"I guess you'll just have to trust me," says Paige, cocking her head again and fluttering her own eyelashes.

Max sighs and then slowly nods.

"Whatcha want from me?" Veronica asks, stepping closer and bouncing on her heels.

Max looks down at his shoes and is quiet for a long time. He's never quiet. His big toe nudges the edge of the step where the carpet is peeling the teeny, tiniest of bits. "Just . . . just be nice to my dad, okay? Since you get to live with him and all."

I suck in a breath. I did *not* expect that one. Veronica just gives her usual shrug. "Easy-peasy. Your dad is the best."

Max nods, still examining the rug. Then he stands, turns, and walks up the steps. I almost feel sort of sorry for him, but when he gets to the top, his evil grin is back as he turns and blows a kiss to Paige. "I'll be waiting, my sweet."

Paige pretend gags until the door clicks closed.

"Okay, so I think we bought his silence. We have four and a half hours until our parents show up. Although we could have way less time if Mrs. G. decides to come down and check on us. We need to find Anna Marie superfast," Paige says.

Duh.

"Word," Veronica agrees.

I fiddle with the strings on the hood of my sweatshirt, pulling them first one way, then the other. I'm trying extra-hard not to think about the fact that we really don't have any solid clues.

After a second, Paige reaches out and touches the bottom hem of my hoodie. "Hold on, you guys. Max isn't the only other person we could ask. Someone else saw us last night."

"Who?" Veronica asks.

Paige points to my sweatshirt. "Follow me!" she orders.

CHAPTER EIGHT

Kobe Bean Bryant

"I can't believe we're gonna do this," I say, but no one answers me. Probably because I said it the entire time it took us to change out of our pajamas and tug on our shoes, and also the whole time Veronica tried to convince me to let her draw on an eyebrow using the face paint she brought in case we'd wanted her to teach us how to mime last night. Because "miming is a lost art and the world needs more of us," she claimed.

I may or may not have repeated it a few more times as we made our way from the Guerreros' basement door and around to the front entrance of Anna Marie's next-door neighbor Jake Ribano. *Jake Ribano.* I'm *still* repeating it as we stand on his porch, because I can't help myself. I really *can't* believe we're gonna do this.

Veronica pushes her way past me. "Why isn't anyone pressing the button?"

Paige and I exchange a look. Veronica lives two towns over. She has *no idea* whose doorbell she's about to ring.

"You just . . . You don't understand," I finally say. "It's. Jake. Ribano. He's, like, all dark and mysterious, and he's this loner who skateboards and plays an electric guitar and dresses in all black and wears this skull hoodie everywhere. He's dangerous. I heard a rumor he called in a bomb threat to our school last spring because he'd forgotten to study for a test."

Paige says, "I heard he has a fifth grader make his lunch and drop it off on his porch every morning."

I nod. "I heard that one too. And last year the pool turned fluorescent orange at the start of a swim meet, and someone said they saw Jake leaving school right before that."

I sigh. He really is danger personified. And I . . . am pretty much the opposite. So what if he's gorgeous, with this kind of blue-black hair that falls across his face and bright blue eyes that have actual soul to them?

Veronica shrugs. "Fuzzy from *Get Fuzzy* likes to say, 'Don't judge a book by its cover.' Anyway, whoever he is, you're wearing his sweatshirt, so obviously he saw us at some point last night. Let's find out when!"

I hate that she makes total sense. She reaches up and presses the doorbell. I shiver (I try to tell myself that's it's just from the cool air), and even nothing-phases-me Paige picks at her cuticles while looking everywhere but at the front door.

A gong echoes inside the house. It's a pretty normal house for such a mysterious guy. There's a narrow window to the side of the entrance, and through it I can see a long carpet runner leading to the back of the house, plus a staircase going upstairs. There's an entry table holding a bowl to toss keys into, and a lamp with a sunflower pattern on the shade.

No one comes.

Veronica taps out two long and one short ding on the bell and steps back. Inside, it's still nothing but dark and silence. "Whelp. They're not home," she says, hopping off the porch.

Paige and I share a look that's equal parts disappointment and relief. I really was not prepared for Jake Ribano. We follow Veronica along the shrubs dividing the two yards and slink back through Anna Marie's basement door.

"What now?"

"I bet the chicks need some food," Veronica says. "Do you think they'd like Doritos?"

"Um . . . probably not," Paige answers, slipping her phone from her pocket. "I'll google it and see what they do eat. We probably *should* take care of them while we think of what to do next."

My stomach growls. I personally wouldn't say no to some Doritos. Are there any left? I hunt through the total disaster of a basement until I discover our food stash from last night. There are only crumbs in the Doritos bag, but the bowl of popped popcorn that had Paige's phone only has a tiny bit of Silly String in it now. I also find a bag of Chips Ahoy!— breakfast of champions. I bring both with me for sharing as I follow Veronica into the bathroom. The chicks are all huddled by the drain in the empty tub.

"Oh gross. They've pooped all over."

"It's a natural human biological function," Veronica says.

"True. Even if they're chicks, not humans," I reply.

"Actually, guys, these aren't chicks. They're ducklings," Paige says, coming into the bathroom with her cell phone in hand. "Look at their feet." We peer at them.

We're concentrating on the inside of the bathtub when a noise sounds right behind us.

Squeak!

We all stand up and spin around, trying to see where it's coming from.

Squeak!

With my heart in my throat, I peek behind the toilet and exhale. "Oh! Look!"

I cup my hand, and a tiny ducking waddles into it. Its little webbed feet tickle my palm. He's soooooo sweet. I want to keep him forever. Finally something about this morning that isn't horrible.

"Guys, he's so cute! Look, he's got black feathers instead of yellow! I bet he's been stuck there all morning. I definitely didn't see him when I counted earlier—that makes seventeen. How did you get out of the tub, little guy?"

Paige stares at him with her mouth open. "Ducklings . . ." she says. "One black one . . . Megs, who do you have for science?"

"Mr. Fontana—same as you. And thanks a lot for remembering that I sit three rows behind you!"

"Right, right. Sorry. Who does Anna Marie have?"

"I'm pretty sure she has Miss Shanley. What does this have to do with anything?" I trail my finger along the duckling's downy feathers. They feel like the fuzz on the outside of a peach. Or maybe like the crushed velvet on the dress my mom makes me wear to church whenever the handbell choir performs. The duckling blinks up at me, and my heart completely melts. Total cuteness attack!

I'm barely paying attention to Paige at this point, even when she says, "Because I think I know exactly where these ducklings came from! Miss Shanley's class hatched ducks from eggs last month. I bet these are them! Fiona Brock is in that class, and she told me there was a petition going around to free the ducks from captivity. What if Anna Marie signed the petition? Or did more than signed it? What if she—*we*— actually went through with it . . . last night?"

Well, *now* I'm paying attention. My jaw drops. "You think we *stole* these ducks from school?" It is officially official. I am Dead

Girl Walking. I can't even hold this little duckling anymore—
he's too incriminating. I bend and release him into the tub to
join his brothers and sisters. He utters a tiny and ridiculously
adorable pip-squeaky *quack* in thanks, and my heart squeezes.

"He's so cute," I whisper, mostly to myself.

"He's a she," Veronica states. "Male ducks are silent. No
quacking for them. Also, did you know a group of ducks is
called a raft? True fact."

I stare at Veronica, but Paige chooses to answer my question from before instead.

"Think about it. Where else could they have come from?
And I know one of their ducklings hatched black, because
afterward Matthew Willington told this whole awful ugly
duckling joke at lunch."

I watch the ducklings waddle along the base of the bathtub, trying to climb the walls and slip-sliding down again.
"Whoa."

It hits me that we stole them. *Stole* them. I'm a criminal.
Does that mean there is someone with criminal tendencies
lurking inside me? But I'm always *good*. I wanted last night to
get regular crazy, not law-breaking crazy!

"We need to return them," says Paige.

"You mean sneak *back* into the science classroom? My
mother will murder me. Murder!" Which was bound to happen anyway, but why hasten the process?

"You're always saying that, and yet here you are in one piece. Besides, your mom will murder you worse if we've lost Anna Marie. At least now we have a clue. We need to go to the school and see what else we can find there."

"But it's Saturday. It'll be locked."

"Nope." Paige shakes her head. "Remember what's happening at school later today?"

I look at her with blank eyes, and Paige laughs. "Oh, Megs. Did you sleep through yesterday's pep rally?"

"Right!" Now my eyes get big. "The basketball game against Hillside!" I'd gone home with a slight headache from all the pounding on the bleachers everyone had been doing, but all that energy and excitement had been kind of cool. I can't believe I forgot about it so quickly. Then again, forgetfulness *is* kind of the theme of the morning.

"Kobe Bryant's middle name is Bean," Veronica says. She's scooped up four ducklings from the tub and now has them nestled against different parts of her, including one in the crook of her neck. It's like she's recreating the stuffed animal hideout in Anna Marie's room in duckling form.

"What?" I ask.

Veronica tries to bend down for a fifth duckling while keeping the other four in place. "Kobe Bryant. He's a basketball player. You were talking about basketball. Have you ever had Kobe beef? It's supposed to be far superior to regular steak."

Paige digests this information wordlessly and then picks up her phone again. I manage a small smile before rescuing the duckling trying to escape down Veronica's back.

"It says here they need to be kept really warm," Paige offers, examining the screen on her cell. "It's fine in this bathroom, but we're gonna need to bundle them to get them to the school. Do you think we could get Max to find an old towel for us?"

"Not unless you want to double the length of your lip-lock," I guess.

"I know! We can use my extra bathrobe!" Veronica says.

"Extra? You not only packed a bathrobe for a sleepover, you packed a backup, too?" Paige asks.

"I like to be prepared," Veronica states.

I help Veronica remove a duckling from the bend in her elbow, and place it back in the tub. "I hate to say it, but it's probably gonna get pooped on. Is that okay?"

Veronica shrugs. "Sure. I have two more at home."

The three of us nestle the ducklings carefully inside Veronica's fluffy yellow bathrobe, where all but one of them blend right in against the soft material. Paige tucks the bundle into my backpack, which Veronica slips onto her front so she can keep watch as we walk. Good thing Veronica clearly doesn't mind looking super-odd.

Ten minutes later we're standing in front of my school.

Veronica sticks two fingers inside her mouth and extracts something pulpy and orange, which she then tucks into the bag.

Um . . .

"What is *that*?" Paige asks a second before I can.

"Chewed-up carrots. When you were emptying Meghan's backpack, I borrowed your phone and saw you can supplement duckling food with small bits of veggies. We had the tray of carrot sticks Mrs. Guerrero brought down, which none of us even touched last night—no big mystery because why would anyone eat carrots when they have pizza and Doritos and M&M's?—and if you ask me, Mrs. Guerrero was crazy for—"

"Veronica!" Paige interrupts.

"Yeah?"

"Why are you giving the baby ducks *chewed* carrots?"

"Oh, well, mama birds chew the food for their babies first, and I figured ducks are birds, so they'd probably feel more at home that way."

This noise comes out of my mouth that sounds a lot like a whimper. "Backpacks are washable, aren't they?" I ask in a small voice.

Paige just sighs and looks out across the school's empty parking lots. I only see two cars parked at the very far end of the side lot.

"C'mon, guys. Let's do this."

CHAPTER NINE

Locker Rooms and Incubators

We (plus a backpack full of baby ducklings) stride up to the entrance of West Oak Middle School and rattle the front doors. Um, yeah. Not gonna happen. The school is locked up tight.

"I thought you said it would be open for the game this afternoon?" I'm trying not to sound too accusatory, but I might not be succeeding.

Paige blows her bangs out of her eyes. "I *assumed* it would be. But the game's not until four, so I guess . . ."

Veronica disappears around the corner of the building. She pops her head back, points with two fingers to her own eyes, then at us, and motions with her hand for us to follow. Like we're spies or soldiers or something. Rambo Veronica: on the move. But we don't exactly have another plan B. I take off after her, and Paige saunters along behind me. We creep along the perimeter of the building, yanking on each side door we pass.

Locked.

Locked.

Locked.

We go three-quarters of the way around the building to the last sidewall, where gray cement blocks outline the double doors to the gymnasium's emergency exit. I've only ever been through these doors when we do fire drills. And of course . . . they're locked. From inside the backpack, the baby ducklings make tiny squeaking noises that sound about as hopeless as I feel right now.

"It's no use," I say. "The whole school's locked. What do we do now?" This time, instead of sounding annoyed, I have to fight to keep the whine out of my voice. But really, it *is* a whine-worthy situation. How are we ever going to find Anna Marie if we can't even follow up on the measly clues we have?

Veronica busies herself readjusting the backpack straps on her shoulders as Paige marches up to the very last door on the wall. She gives us a *Here goes nothing* look and then tugs on it with all her strength. It opens so easily, she stumbles back and lands on her butt in the dirt as we all gape at the door. Veronica shoves it closed.

"What are you doing?" Paige screeches, popping up and dusting off her black skinny jeans.

"Peek in first. Make sure the coast is clear," Veronica says with a shrug. "Junior Detective basics." She eases the metal door open again, then sticks her head inside and swivels it left, then right. "Looks clear to me. I think it's the locker room."

Paige and I follow her inside cautiously. As soon as I feel the warm heat on my cheeks, I sniff and then wrinkle my nose.

"Definitely the *boys'* one!" I say.

The smell is pretty much the opposite of Jake's sweat-shirt's soap-and-mint boy smell. This is stinky socks and BO all the way. Ick. I pinch my nose and try to breathe through my mouth. I also try really hard not to think about the fact that *OMG, we're in the boys' locker room.* Where boys are usually . . . you know.

In front of us is a long bank of green metal lockers, leading to the corner of yet another row. In the distance I hear the sounds of a shower. My eyes bug out of my head.

"Um, guys. I know we shouldn't be in the school at all, but I *definitely* don't think we should be in *here*!"

"So true." Paige shudders. "Let's go!"

We wind our way through a maze of lockers, but the shower noises just seem to get closer. Oh no. No, no, no, no. My heart is thudding so loudly, it sounds like a marching band.

But what's even worse is when those shower noises stop altogether.

"Run!" Paige whisper-yells, and the three of us book it around the corner.

I spot an exit sign over a door and aim for it. We burst

through into an empty hallway, panting heavily. Close one! That could have been mega-awkward. Veronica checks on the ducklings while we catch our breaths. "Everyone is good. Waddleworth looks a little motion sick though."

Waddleworth? I mouth to Paige.

"We should stay on the move," Paige says, pushing off the wall and leading the way to the eighth-grade wing. We pass the inside entrance to the gym, where the walls are covered in painted posters cheering on the basketball team. We creep past the vending machine with its sugar-free juices and healthy snacks, and then the empty cafeteria, minus the regular school-day smells of goopy lasagna and soggy broccoli.

We're just about to turn the corner, when we hear whistling. Paige holds out her hand to stop us.

Of course, Veronica walks right into her.

Paige sucks in a breath and then puts a finger to her lips. She peers around the corner and then back at us. "Janitor," she whispers. "He just went into Mr. Fontana's room, pushing a mop."

"Oh great. That's right next to Miss Shanley's," I answer. "Do you think he already did hers, or is hers next? Which way was he coming from?"

Paige shrugs. "I couldn't tell."

The three of us stick in place, waiting, like our feet are in cement. Paige acts as lookout on the eighth-grade corridor while I dart glances over my shoulder at all that empty hall-way behind us. I pray hard that no one will come around the corner and spot us. It's so quiet that even our deep breaths seem to echo. I can't remember ever being in our school when there wasn't all kinds of talking and slamming lockers and shoes scuffing on the floor. This kind of silence is super-eerie. Even the ducklings must sense something, because they're still too. To calm my nerves, I start counting in my head. I do this a lot when teachers are passing back tests, and it works. Sometimes. I'm all the way up to 146 before Paige whispers.

"He just came out! Now he's going across the hall into Miss Ross's room," she reports.

"What do we do? We can't keep standing here in the middle of the school! What if someone sees us? We'll get expelled!" I say.

Paige bursts out laughing (quietly of course), and I put both hands on my hips. "I'm really sorry," she says. "It's just when you're upset, your eyebrow goes up, and, well, it's kind of funny to see just one wiggling. Oh man, that was really rude. Forgive?"

My hands fly to my face, and my fingers explore the smooth skin above my eye. I'd almost managed to forget about it again. Drat, Paige! Although it's going to be this times eighty-seven classmates come school on Monday. I wish I'd worn the knit cap Veronica had offered me before we left Anna Marie's, but I was worried it would make me look way too much like a burglar, and the last thing I wanted to do before breaking into school was dress the part. Um, plus it had a picture of the Wiggles on it. So there's that.

Maybe getting expelled wouldn't be such a bad thing, after all. Maybe my mom would let me wait until my eyebrow grew back before finding me a new school to attend.

And, hey, if we get caught and I get sent to juvie, maybe I can convince the scary teens who are there for serious stuff that my eyebrow is some kind of sign of how tough I am, the way prisoners tattoo teardrops on their faces to show they've murdered someone. Then at least they'd leave me alone.

I'm pretty deep into my jailhouse fantasy when a duckling lets loose a tiny quack from the backpack and snaps me out of it. Paige is still peeking over at me with sorry eyes, waiting to see if I forgive her. Of course I do. Paige can be a little bit insensitive sometimes, but she doesn't mean anything by it. And besides, having Paige stick up for me at school on Monday is possibly the only thing that could maybe keep the mocking at a minimum. Paige is Popular with a capital *P*, and if Paige says my solo eyebrow is cool, chances are, by the end of the day, half the girls at school will be volunteering to shave their own off.

I smile and shrug, and Paige pulls me in for a hug before

saying, "We have to get down that wing. Let's make a run for Miss Shanley's room on the count of three. Veronica, it's the fourth door on the left."

Veronica hums distractedly, her hands in the backpack of ducklings.

"One, two, *three*," Paige whispers, and I take off running on my tiptoes. I follow Paige into the science classroom, skidding around the corner and narrowly avoiding a desk with a chair stacked on it.

Neither of us have Miss Shanley, but her science classroom looks pretty much like ours. A giant periodic table poster covers one wall, and a framed print above Miss Shanley's desk says in block letters, NEVER TRUST AN ATOM. THEY MAKE UP EVERYTHING. Hardy har. In the corner, a skeleton wearing a top hat dangles from a closet door.

The other corner has a deep plastic tub lined with towels and lit by a heating lamp.

A very *empty* plastic tub.

I glance at it and then back at Paige and Veronica.

Wait.

Where's Veronica?

I make my way over to the doorway. "I don't see her!"

"Well, we can't return ducklings without, ya know, any ducklings." Paige puts a hand on her hip the way she always does when she's annoyed. "If she gets us busted, I swear . . ."

"We have to split up and look for her in the other class-rooms," I whisper. "Wait! Get down!"

The janitor comes out of the English classroom and leans his mop against a locker. Phew—that was close! Hold on, is that a Taylor Swift song he's whistling? Weird (but kinda funny). He pauses in the hallway, looking down the corridor before hitching his pants up and setting off to his left. I tuck myself flat against the doorway and watch as he pushes into the teachers' bathroom, leaving his bucket in the middle of the hall.

"We have a minute or two. He's in the bathroom. You go that way, and I'll look over there." I point across the hall.

When Paige nods, I race to our drama room and slip inside the hanging rack of costumes all set up for next month's production of *Annie*. An orange wig of curls hangs over a hanger and tickles my nose. I swat it away. It would be a *disaster* to sneeze at a moment like this!

I scan the room but don't see any signs of an awkward girl, and I definitely don't see any clusters of ducklings. Herd of ducklings? Flock of ducklings? What did Veronica say it was? I shake my head. *Not important, Meghan. Find Veronica, return the ducks, and look for clues that might help you find Anna Marie. In that order.*

I abandon my hiding spot in the classroom and move to the doorway, where I slowly stick my head out into the still-empty hallway. I suck in a deep breath, getting ready to dash back into Miss Shanley's classroom. Maybe Paige found Veronica, and they're returning the ducklings right this very second. A flash of movement across the hall catches my eye, and in the split second before I register what I'm seeing, my heart stops as completely as it did the time I couldn't bring myself to jump off the ski lift when I reached the station at the top. Unlike then, when I had to be pulled off by my legs as I swung around the turnstile, this time my heart recovers immediately. It's Paige, easing out of a classroom, holding Veronica by the arm.

I sigh with relief. Paige spots me and grins, and we take a step out of our doorways when a noise at the other end of the hallway snaps our necks around. The door to the teachers' bathroom is opening! I duck back inside the drama room and pray so, so hard that Paige and Veronica did the same in the science room. I can hardly bear to look.

I hear whistling getting closer and then the sounds of a mop being pushed in and then lifted out of a bucket. I try counting again to calm down, but it doesn't help the way it did before. My heart keeps racing like it's playing catch-up in Mario Kart. But if the janitor saw anything, he wouldn't be whistling. He'd be shouting. So he *didn't* notice us! Now I just have to cross my fingers he isn't headed for the drama classroom next. The whistling stops.

I count to twenty again and then screw up all my

courage to peek into the hallway again. All is quiet. Should I stay? Should I go? What are Paige and Veronica doing right now? I hesitate in the doorway for a few seconds, and then I just . . . go. I dash across the hall to Miss Shanley's class, exhaling when I see Paige and Veronica already inside. They're busy placing the tiny ducklings back into the plastic tub.

"Couldn't I just keep Waddleworth?" Veronica is saying. "Who would notice?"

Paige slips the backpack off Veronica's shoulders. "We need to find Anna Marie, not babysit a duckling all day. Why don't Megs and I do this part, and you stand lookout in the doorway?"

Veronica lowers her shoulders and crosses the room.

"You should be nicer to her," I say to Paige as we gently return the rest of the ducklings and refill their water supply from a bottle sitting next to the tub.

"I know, I know. I'm not trying to be mean. She just doesn't really pick up on any signals, so I kind of have to be blunt, ya know? Besides, we can't let her *keep* one of the ducklings!"

I nod but keep quiet, and eventually Paige says, "Fine. I'll try harder."

That's all I was saying to begin with.

When we're satisfied the little guys are comfortable and safe, we turn back to the doorway.

But Veronica isn't there.

CHAPTER TEN

Do Janitors in Japan Play Unicycle Floor Hockey?

"Did you know, in Japan, schools don't have janitors? The kids do all the cleaning every day because Buddhist traditions associate cleanliness with morality. Isn't that cool? Well, not for you, obviously. You'd be out of work if you moved there, huh?"

I watch in horror as Veronica walks in the opposite direction from us, yammering away to the janitor. Um, say *what*? What is she doing?

I can't see his face, but he sounds pretty annoyed when he says, "That's great, kid. But you still haven't answered me. What are you doing here?"

Veronica hops over wet mop marks on the floor. "Oh. That's easy. I'm returning this backpack I found outside."

The janitor mops back and forth, from locker bank to locker bank, crisscrossing the hallway. "Doesn't explain what you're doing, wandering the classrooms and . . ."

The voices trail off as the pair round the corner. I steal one last look at the ducklings, happily tumbling around in the plastic tub, then at Paige. "We have to follow them," I whisper. "If he calls the police or something . . ."

"I know."

We creep from the classroom and down the hallway. We stay a good distance behind Veronica and the mopping janitor, ducking into each classroom doorway as we make our way along the hallway. Veronica continues to chatter away, seeming completely "whatever" about getting busted.

Oh. My. God. I think he's walking her to the main office. I'm sure my eyes are completely frantic as I try to will Paige to look at me. When she does, I make hand motions to indicate Veronica is about to walk into the Hornet's Nest (which is Anna Marie's nickname for Principal Wexman's office).

Surely, she won't be here on a Saturday, though. Even principals get a day off, right?

Paige doesn't seem to get what I'm trying to say with my hands, and she makes a face, then darts into the next doorway. I see the exact moment she realizes which hall we're about to turn down. Her whole body freezes.

Up ahead I can just hear the indistinct sounds of Veronica chattering away at the janitor. What is she *doing*? Why couldn't she have just stayed in the classroom like we'd told her?

I'm afraid to peek around the corner. But I have to. My

heart zooms right into my throat when I do because *Veronica is going into the office.*

And holding the door open for her is our principal!

We're dead. Or expelled. Or expelled and then dead.

At this point I'm tempted to throw my hands up and turn myself in. Maybe I'd get brownie points for offering myself up. But Paige tugs my shirt and whispers, "Let's sneak closer."

My brain is whirring with so many different disaster scenarios that involve my parents—who think I'm blissfully sleeping away the morning at Anna Marie's—getting called by the principal to come pick me up at school. Or worse, what if Principal Wexman involves the police? We *are* on school property when we're not supposed to be and, even though we didn't *technically* break in because the door was unlocked, Principal Wexman isn't one for technicalities. Last year she suspended Sarah Mills for packing a butter knife in her lunch bag so she could spread peanut butter on her apple slices, because our school has a zero tolerance policy on "weapons."

But in the midst of all these horrific thoughts, I don't have the mental capacity to make any decisions, so I just follow along as Paige creeps closer. Within seconds we're right outside the door to the office, which is open just wide enough that we can hear what's happening inside.

"So nice of you to return the backpack, but I'm curious how you got in? The school is closed until the game."

Yikes. Principal Wexman's voice is all gravelly and serious.

"Tried the door and it was open, so how could I know it was off-limits?"

"Which door was open?"

"Um, you know, I can't be positive. I'm so turned around with all these hallways. This sure is a big school. I'm e-schooled, so the only hallways I have to walk are between my bedroom and the living room, except if you count the one to the bathroom, which I guess you'd have to since I use that approximately seven times a day. Mom says I have the tini-est bladder known to man, even though I'm not a man. Any-way, it's really a nice school you have here. I bet I'd like it. Do you have a unicycle floor hockey team? Cuz that'd be a deal breaker for me coming here if you don't. . . ."

If I weren't about to soil my pants, I'd be rolling on the floor laughing right now. I wonder what Principal Wexman is making of Veronica. Next to me, Paige's shoulders start shak-ing, and she stuffs her fist into her mouth.

"Uh, no, we don't have a team for unicycle . . . Did you say floor hockey? Ahem. No. But our basketball team is only a few games away from going to the state championship."

Oh, this is actually good. If Veronica can get Principal Wexman going on about our basketball team, we might be okay. The woman is obsessed.

But I should know better. This is Veronica we're talking about. Sure enough, the next thing she says is, "You should really consider unicycle floor hockey. It's a great workout. Extra-good for balance. If you want, I can write to the International Unicycling Federation and get you the info you'd need to get accredited."

At this Paige can't hold back anymore. She lets out this noise that sounds like a cross between a dog bark and a cough. All is quiet in the office and then . . .

"One moment please," says a gravelly voice.

I grab Paige's shirt. My eyes are popping out of my head like a cartoon character's. Heels click-click across the floor, and I can't bear to look. I bury my face in Paige's shirt.

Someone clears her throat very, very close to me. I steal a peek.

"Hello, girls," says my principal.

CHAPTER ELEVEN

White Hair and Carrot-Covered Fingers

I once read about people who suffer an extreme fright, and then their hair turns white overnight. I sincerely hope that doesn't happen to me, because it's going to be bad enough being the girl with one eyebrow.

"Hello, Principal Wexman," Paige says brightly, as if nothing at all is wrong and we make a habit of skulking around the school hallways on our days off.

"H-hi," I manage. I can't look our principal in the eyes. I'm sure I seem beyond guilty.

"May I inquire as to what you ladies are doing hiding in a doorway outside my office?" Her voice sounds less scratchy and more sticky-sweet, but I'm not fooled one little bit.

"Oh well, we could hear you had a visitor, and we didn't want to interrupt." Still Paige is able to keep her voice all sunshine and innocence. *How does she do that?* "So we were just waiting politely."

"Mmm" is the reply. Principal Wexman doesn't sound like she's buying this. "And just what brings you to West Oak on a Saturday?"

"Meghan," Paige says. I swallow hard. Did she just say *my* name? Paige reaches behind her back and finds my hand, never dropping her smile. She squeezes.

"Meghan here lost her backpack in all the excitement of the pep rally yesterday, and we figured we'd try to find it. We checked her locker and took a quick peek around, so now we were headed to you to see if it ended up in the lost and found. Speaking of the pep rally, what do you think our chances are in the game later?"

Paige knows *exactly* how to distract Principal Wexman, and for a second I think it's going to work.

She takes a breath as if to answer us, but then her forehead wrinkles.

"I don't understand why everyone thinks they are at liberty to roam the hallways of this school when, clearly, it is not open to students." She darts a glance back at Veronica, who's now in the hallway too. Principal Wexman's gaze falls on the backpack in Veronica's hand, and she purses her lips.

"I take it this is this missing item?" she asks me.

"I— It— Um," I stammer.

"*Yes!* You've found it, Principal Wexman. Thank you so,

so much! Meghan here has been superworried she wouldn't get to finish her math assignment before Monday, and you know what a good student she is. She's *very* dedicated to her schoolwork." Paige is laying it on a little thick, but Principal Wexman doesn't seem to notice. She reaches her hand for the backpack Veronica holds out and then passes it silently to me. But just before I grab it, her grasp tightens.

"I suppose just because school is not in session doesn't mean we shouldn't follow proper protocol. Lost-and-found items have to be verified. Can you tell me what the contents of this backpack are to prove it's yours?"

"I— Uh— Um." This is never going to work if I can't spit out more than syllables. I take a deep breath and say, "Um, a notebook and, um, a math book and . . . and a calculator."

I know full well none of those items are going to be in the backpack, but I can't figure out what else to say. This is a disaster.

Principal Wexman slides open the zipper and peers inside. Her nose crinkles as she tugs a corner of Veronica's fluffy yellow bathrobe out. She levels me with a questioning look and then stuffs her hand back in.

"Huh. Weird," Paige says right away. "Someone must be playing a prank on us. You know what: I'll bet it's those Hillside kids. They love to ramp up the rivalry before a big game, right? I say we don't stand for this."

Principal's Wexman's eyes narrow, and she mutters, "Hillside," under her breath. As much as Principal Wexman loves basketball, that's how much she loathes Hillside Heights.

Hillside Heights is the hoity-toity private school that backs up to West Oak and also shares our athletic fields, making us the worst kinds of rivals. We have regular school grounds; they have a "campus." Never mind that half of it consists of the same exact soccer field and tennis courts.

Unlike West Oak, which is mostly made out of concrete blocks, Hillside Heights is old-school, literally. Its buildings (yup, there are more than one) are ancient-looking red brick.

Principal Wexman hates that they have a state-of-the-art computer lab and that their principal gets to live in a huge mansion on the edge of campus. But most of all, she especially despises the fact that their basketball team has stolen the state championship from us for three years running. I can tell even the thought of Hillside playing a prank on us has her good and distracted. She pulls her hand out of my backpack. It's covered in mushed-up carrot bits. A small fuzzy feather clings to one of the pieces.

"Wow. Those Hillside kids are diabolical. I think this warrants a call to their coach," Paige says, all innocence. She could give Max a run for his money.

Principal Wexman's eyes narrow, and she nods once before

turning from us. She takes a few steps toward her office before facing us again. "Please use the front doors to exit, girls. I'll have the janitor lock up behind you. Thank you for bringing this tomfoolery to my attention."

She gestures to the row of doors right beside the main office and hovers as we race over to them. They must only lock from the outside because they push right open, and we burst into the sunshine. As soon as the metal doors click shut behind us, Paige sinks to her butt on the cement steps.

"That could have been a total disaster!" she says, clasping her side and laughing.

"I wasn't scared," says Veronica, a bland expression on her face.

I want to laugh, from relief more than anything else, but the inside of my head is still buzzing and my heart is racing too fast to do much of anything but slump down beside Paige. Immediately she stands and holds out her hand.

"Let's get out of sight while we figure out what to do next." She pulls me up and walks us over to the corner of the building, away from any windows or the parking lot, where she lets me drop down like a rag doll again. I swear, it's like my bones turned to jelly back there in that hallway.

Paige plops down next to me. Veronica does too, sitting crisscross-applesauce style in the grass. "So, we're all fine, thankfully, but we barely had any time in the classroom to look for more clues. Which leaves us with exactly zero ideas of where our best friend is," Paige says.

She pulls out her phone and flips it around so we can see: 8:25.

We wasted almost a whole hour getting to school and returning the ducks, and we're no closer to finding Anna Marie. In fact, it feels like we're even further than ever from finding her. Pickup time is looming closer and closer. We are so dead.

All three of us stare off into space, lost in our own thoughts. I'm mostly trying to imagine the exact shade of purple my mother's face is gonna turn when she shows up at the Guerreros' house at noon.

Eventually Paige says, "Where'd you come up with unicycle floor hockey?"

Veronica unties and reties her sneaker laces. "Because I play it. Duh."

Paige and I exchange glances over Veronica's head. I try to make my voice all gentle when I say, "Um, no offense, Veronica, but do you mean you wish it were a sport so you could play it?" At least I'm getting my voice back.

Veronica scoffs. "Nooooo. I mean I *actually* play it. Every Tuesday night at the Y in my town. It's a thing. Google it. Anyway, right now it's just me and three other homeschooled kids, and we mostly just scrimmage because we haven't been able to find a whole lot of other people who can ride a unicycle, but Kevin—I mean, Anna Marie's dad—says he's gonna help give lessons after the wedding. I'm gonna try to talk AM into learning so we can practice on the weekends she's visiting us."

I don't want to break it to Veronica that Anna Marie has been known to trip over air, so the idea of her on a unicycle is, well, pretty laughable.

Paige says, "I guess it's no weirder than cheerleading. Did you hear some of the cheers they had at the pep rally yesterday, Megs?"

Who can think about pep rallies at a time like this? I open my mouth to say so, but Veronica speaks first. "Ooh. I've always wanted to be on a cheerleading squad."

Paige blinks several times, fast. "*You* want to be a cheerleader?" I narrow my eyes and try to convey *Be nice!* with them, but, as usual, Veronica seems completely oblivious to Paige's tone.

"Oh, not to cheer," she says. "To be the school mascot. I mean *a* school mascot, since my homeschool is population one, and I don't need any help getting enthusiastic about it. Do you think schools ever choose nonstudents to be their mascots?"

Paige shakes her head in disbelief, but I'm happy to hear that at least her voice is pleasant when she says, "I . . . I really don't know, Veronica."

"Do you know how to do a roundoff? All the mascots I see on TV are always doing roundoffs. I think I might need to know how to do one to get the job."

Paige sighs. "Yes, I know how to do a roundoff."

"Could you teach me? Pretty please? Oh, Paige, puh-leaze!"

Paige looks at me. I know this is probably the last thing we should be doing right now, but I shrug and say, "It's not like we have any brilliant ideas for where to look for Anna Marie. Maybe being upside down will get the blood rushing to your brain, and you'll think of something brilliant."

Paige smirks, but she stands. Veronica jumps into place next to her and carefully copies every move as Paige points one foot and then raises both hands in the air. When Paige executes a perfect roundoff, I can't help it.

I shriek.

Immediately I throw my hands over my mouth.

"Geez, Megs! Are you trying to get Principal Wexman out here?" Paige asks.

Veronica, meanwhile, attempts her own roundoff and lands with her butt on the grass. Paige reaches down to give Veronica a hand up, but she keeps her eyes on me as I point to her. My mouth keeps opening and closing, but nothing is coming out. Eventually I manage, "Lift your shirt."

"What? I'm not flashing you, Meghan Alcott!"

"No, just a little. When you cartwheeled your shirt came up and . . ."

Paige turns and pulls her shirt up just a little. "Blood!"

Paige tries twisting her head around to her back, but she can't see the spot I'm gesturing to. Her voice is wobbly when she asks, "I'm bleeding?"

I nod, but just as fast I shake my head. "No, I mean, not anymore. It's all dried up."

Veronica approaches Paige, then kneels down on the ground and puts her face right next to Paige's back. She leans in close and . . . *licks* Paige's skin! Paige squeals and then jumps forward while I yell (quietly), "Veronica!"

"Did you just *lick* me?" Paige asks, tugging her shirt back down.

"Just as I thought," Veronica says calmly. "It's not blood."

"Did you just *lick* me?" Paige asks again.

"What is it?" I ask.

Paige spins to me. "Megs, the girl *licked* me!"

"I know! So gross, but . . . if it's not blood, what *is* it then, Veronica?"

CHAPTER TWELVE

Flutes and Batons and Tubas, Oh My!

Veronica places her feet hip-width apart and crosses her arms over her chest, looking very self-satisfied. "It's paint," she states.

"Paint? How do you know what paint tastes like?" Paige asks. "Never mind—I don't want to know." Then she bunches her shirt ends in one hand and twists again to try to glimpse whatever the heck it is on her back.

Veronica just shrugs. "Definitely paint. Maroon paint."

Okay, that's just weird.

Where would Paige have gotten maroon paint on herself? I sit on the ground, my chin in my hands. *Think, think, think.* Veronica steps close to Paige again (I catch Paige flinch) and starts circling her, squinting as she moves around her in a careful circle.

"What are you doing?" Paige asks.

"I'm looking to see if you have any more of it on you. Maybe that could help us figure out where it came from."

Paige looks ready to blast her, but she snaps her jaw shut and mutters, "That's actually not a bad idea." She holds her shirt above her belly button and spins slowly.

Veronica purses her lips together in concentration and then reaches forward to tug Paige's top off her shoulder. "Aha!"

This time even Paige can see the streak of orange paint. "Oh!"

"Orange and maroon . . . orange and maroon . . . Are you guys thinking what I'm thinking?" Veronica asks with a smile.

"If you're also thinking, *Why am I prepped for a tribal ceremony?*, then yes," Paige replies.

I have to fight to keep from laughing.

Veronica sounds all smug when she says, "Where's the only place you'll find those two colors combined?"

Paige cocks her head, thinking, and then shrugs. "I give up."

I do too.

Veronica motions for us to follow her around the corner to the front of the school, where the entrance has a giant banner stretched across it. It says, THE WEST OAK WARRIORS WILL CRUSH THE HILLSIDE HEIGHTS HAVOCKING HEDGE-HOGS! The words *West Oak* are painted in our school colors of royal blue and white, while *Hillside Heights* is painted in their school colors.

Orange and maroon.

"Oh! You think . . . ," Paige whispers.

"Orange and maroon are not very complimentary colors. Opposites on a color wheel are optimal combinations," Veronica says.

"I think it's definitely worth investigating," I add. "It's better than anything else we have, and parent pickup time is ticking closer."

We cut across the fields between our two schools, and my mind moves even faster than my feet. How on earth are we gonna find clues here? Will the school be locked up as tight as ours was (well, at first anyway)? We already tested our luck with one instance of breaking and entering today. Are we really contemplating a second one?

But then an image of Anna Marie floats in front of my face. It's from last spring when we were at my house for a study session leading up to a quiz, and we decided we needed a break. Because it was a science test we were studying for, Anna Marie and I rewrote the lyrics of "Defying Gravity" from our favorite play, *Wicked*, to make it "Defining Gravity" (*I think I'll try, defining gravity. And you can't grade me down*) and choreographed a whole dance to match. When we put both together and performed it in front of my mirror, we laughed so hard, my ribs still hurt the next morning.

I have to do *whatever* it takes to find my friend.

My energy comes rushing back, and I grab on to Paige and Veronica. Together we run the length of the last field, circle to the front of the main building, and stride up the sidewalk to the doors. But before we get a single foot on the stairs, the sound of yelling stops us in our tracks. It's coming from the side of the building, where a sign points to the faculty parking lot. Even though we hadn't been hiding before, the sound of people sends us right up along the wall of the building. We creep against the side, and the branches from the bushes all along the edges tickle my legs. I'm first in our line, so I peek around the corner. Five kids in maroon-and-orange band uniforms are having some kind of fight. A loud one!

Paige pulls on my (well, Jake's) sweatshirt to get my attention and then points to a gap in the hedge where we can hide and spy. Once we're all tucked in there, we can't actually see very much, but we can definitely still hear every word. The kids aren't making any effort to keep their voices down.

"Yeah, but if *you'd* been here to watch over it, this never would have—"

"What do you mean, if I'd been here? You were the one who left the second Kelsey Tagent said she needed help tuning her bass!"

"Yeah, well. It was *Kelsey Tagent*!"

"I know, dude, and props for that, but you had one duty and you—"

"Look, I'm not the one who put the thing up on wheels, which made it super-easy to—"

"How else were we supposed to move Hedgie around? He's eight feet tall! Get real!"

"I'm just saying, if it weren't on wheels . . ."

"You guys! Why are we fighting with each other? Is that helping anything? Obi-Wan Ke-*no*-be, it's not!"

I have to stifle a laugh at the expression (which I might be totally stealing in the near future), but my attention is diverted by Veronica, who is waving a hand under her nose. Her eyes are watery, and she's scrunching up her face.

Omigosh, is she about to—

A-a-achoo!

Yup, she is.

Veronica sneezes again.

Then three more times.

I make a desperate face at her, but all Veronica does is shrug and whisper, "I always sneeze in sevens."

Achoo!

Five kids in band uniforms get suspiciously quiet. Paige, Veronica, and I hold perfectly still, crouching down in the bushes, and I use my best Jedi mind skills to will them not to come investigate. I also will my knees not to wobble.

Neither command works. There's rustling right on the other side of our bushes, and then the head of a boy appears over the hedge. He pokes a silver baton wrapped in orange and maroon ribbons into the leaves.

"Ouch!" I cry when the end of it jabs me in the shoulder.

Achoo!

Veronica whispers, "Number seven!" Like *that's* what's important right now. I stick my hands up as if I'm under arrest, and shimmy out of the bushes. Paige and Veronica follow me, and the three of us stand in front of part of the Hillside Heights marching band, while I feverishly try to find a realistic-sounding excuse for our spy mission.

But in the end, the band kids speak first. Or shout, I should say. "It's you!" one accuses, pointing a finger at us.

I raise my eyebrow (singular). "It's you, who?" I ask.

"You! The ones who stole our float! You have some nerve coming here! Are you back to laugh at us? Where is he? Go get him right now!" This comes from a short girl carrying her flute like a weapon and looking supervillainy in spite of the tassels on her uniform buttons.

Paige's and Veronica's eyebrows (of course *they* each have two) are up in the air now also. "What are you guys even talking about? We've never seen you before in our lives." Paige doesn't sound scared in the slightest, as per usual. The whole blood-on-her-back thing might have freaked her out, but a bunch of band kids definitely don't. I wish I could be half as calm—but I'm pretty much freaking out. The only people I'm used to getting yelled at by are my parents, and even that doesn't happen very often. Mom is more of the low-voiced, guilt-trip type.

These kids are definitely yelling. "You came here last night, waited for us to be distracted, and then rolled our Hedgie the Havocking Hedgehog away! Give him back!" the girl with the flute screeches.

I'm pretty sure if I live to be a hundred and sixteen, I will never hear a more ridiculous sentence uttered. But what does it *mean*?

"*What* is a Hedgie the Havocking Hedgehog?" Paige asks.

A boy whose maroon uniform pants are so obviously too small that they show a strip of leg above his sock line answers her. "Hedgie is the giant hedgehog float we've been building all week. We were *supposed* to ride into the gym on it today for our half-time performance at the basketball game. That is, until *you* stole it."

"We didn't steal your float!" I protest. Finally I'm getting some of my nerve back because no way am I taking the blame for something I didn't even do, and I'm not letting my friends get falsely accused either.

"A group of hedgehogs is called a prickle," Veronica informs us.

The band kids' jaws drop open, though they quickly snap shut. Flute Girl steps forward, shaking her instrument at us.

But then she tucks it into one pant pocket (where more than half of it pokes out) and extracts a cell phone from the other. "Well, we're just worried about *one* hedgehog," she says. "And if you didn't steal our float, then how do you explain *this*?"

Paige, Veronica, and I huddle around the phone as the girl presses play on a YouTube video.

At first all we can see is a giant hulking form in the darkness, rolling slowly.

"What is this, like, a surveillance video?" Paige asks.

"No! Be quiet and watch!" Flute Girl orders. *Um, bossy much?*

On-screen, the shape passes under a light in the parking lot, and I gasp. On one end of a wheeled platform that holds a crazy-tall papier-mâché hedgehog shaking his fist are Paige and Veronica, pulling on a piece of rope. Pushing from behind is . . . me.

My stomach feels all hollow, and my mouth tastes like sandpaper. I can convince myself that we rescued the ducklings with good intentions and that "breaking in" to school today to return them was also for a legitimate cause, but we had zero reason to steal a hedgehog float. I really *am* a criminal.

I'm still trying to process this when the camera pulls back a little, and I can make out two people helping me to push.

Anna Marie!

And Jake Ribano.

"Anna Marie! She was with us then. This is a huge break-through!" says Paige.

"Jake Ribano," I say breathlessly. Wow, Jake Ribano *was* with us last night, and now we have undeniable proof. I hug his sweatshirt tightly around me. I can't even wrap my head around this much information at once.

The girl with the flute snatches back her phone. "So, you can see we have all the evidence we need to prosecute you. You are *b-u-s-t-e-d*." She spells each letter and practically spits the *d*.

"Look," Paige says, dropping her arm from Veronica's shoulders. "I know you have this video and all, but you have to believe us: We don't remember any of what happened last night. None of it."

The skinny boy with the baton snorts. "No, *you* have to believe *us*. We don't care. We want our float back, and we want it back now."

Paige throws up her hands. "We don't know where your ridiculous float is. We wish we did, because we'd definitely make sure you got your, er, Hedgie, back safe and sound, but we don't and we can't. We're really sorry."

"Oh no, blondie," says the boy with the floodwater pants. "You may be sorry now, but you're not even close to how sorry you're gonna be if we don't have our float back in time for the game. But I think we're gonna get it back way faster than that, don't you, guys?"

The other band members cackle. Flute Girl even rubs her hands together.

"See, we've been trying to figure out all morning how to contact you, which you made too easy by coming right back to the scene of your crime. You may have thought you could just sit in those bushes and laugh at all the chaos you caused, but we're the one's laughing now because we have something of yours. Something you *really* want—even more than we want our float, I'm guessing."

I turn a puzzled face to Paige and Veronica, and then my eyes grow big. They have Anna Marie! "You have her?"

"And you're not getting her back until we have our float!" The boy wearing floods grins wickedly at us.

"But we don't know where your float *is*!" This is so not fair. They can't expect us to produce something we've never seen before (that we can remember), and they really, really can't keep Anna Marie hostage like this. We could call the cops!

Except I remember the video showing us committing a theft, so I keep my mouth shut.

The boy looks me up and down with scorn. "Well, I'd say you're sufficiently motivated to find it, wouldn't you?" His band friends giggle as they surround us, hands on their hips.

The one with the fancy baton speaks next. "You have

one hour. We'll be waiting behind the Dunkin' Donuts on Hillside Ave. We expect to see a Havocking Hedgehog roll up then."

They turn and march away to the far end of the parking lot, where instrument cases lie in a jumbled pile. Veronica shakes her fist at their backs.

Paige and I grab hands. "We have to find it. We can't leave Anna Marie alone with those . . . those *band people* for even one second more than we have to!" I say.

"Do you know I can play the tuba?" Veronica asks.

CHAPTER THIRTEEN

Hedgie the Havocking Hedgehog

"Okay, so now, instead of searching for a missing girl, we're searching for a missing hedgehog?" I shake my head at how crazy this entire morning has been. Baby ducklings and Silly String and a shaved eyebrow and, seriously, could this day get any weirder? But at least we found Anna Marie.

Sort of.

We approach Anna Marie's house from the street behind it and creep through the yard to the Guerreros' back door, which opens into the basement.

I push open the door as softly as I can, happy to see it's as dark in there as when we left it. The pillows are still tucked into our sleeping bags to make it look like we're peacefully snoring inside. And, honestly, if Mrs. Guerrero had turned on a light and seen the disaster we'd made of the basement, she'd have yanked us straight out of our sleeping bags for a serious talking to. I mean, it's Level 27 Nuclear. The fact that the pillows are still in place can mean only one thing: no one's been down here.

Phew! It's nine thirty, which technically could still be considered early by sleepover standards. I figure we probably have another hour, at least, before Mrs. Guerrero gets suspicious about how late we're sleeping in and comes down to investigate.

Except we have waaaaay less than an hour to find a missing hedgehog float. The walk/run back to Anna Marie's took us fourteen precious minutes. But at least we formulated a plan while we went. It's not elaborate. In fact, it's pretty super-simple, and it's called Ask Jake Ribano because he's basically our only hope at this point. According to the video the marching band kids showed us, he'd been front and center (well, more like back and center, since he was helping me push from behind) when we were stealing Hedgie. With his reputation, it was probably *his* idea in the first place. Either way, he helped us steal it, so he must know where we stashed it (where *would* one "stash" a giant hedgehog?). He *has* to know where it is now. He just has to.

If not, we're toast.

This time the door swings open before we even have a chance to debate who will push the doorbell. A very smiley Jake Ribano is on the other side.

Um, weird.

Jake is usually all silent, bad-boy broody, not grinning like a kid who just adopted a puppy. What is going on here? Of all the strange things we've seen so far today, this is possibly the strangest of all.

"About time!" he says, smiling right at me. I take a step back and crash into Paige, who also stumbles and practically falls off the porch.

"Hi! I'm Veronica," she offers.

Jake crinkles his nose in confusion and says, "Um, yeah, I know. Hi." He looks over her shoulder at me and, I swear, it's like his eyes soften. Um . . . "Hey," he says gently, almost *shyly*.

I would be completely busy dying if I weren't so consumed with trying not to hyperventilate over how cute Jake looks in his flannel button-down shirt and corduroys. Neither of which are black, I note. This day gets weirder still. Is it possible this is all one realllllllly long dream?

Nightmare. Dream.

Well, nightmare, because my best friend is missing, but definitely dream when Jake looks at me—*me!*—like he is.

"Ah . . ." But that's all I can manage, because my brain and mouth somehow refuse to connect. I can't look away either, so I just stand there, gaping like a fish.

Paige clears her throat, and both Jake and I blink.

"So sorry to bother you, Jake," she says, "but we're a little confused about some things that may or may not have happened last night, and we were, uh, hoping you could shed some light."

He grins at us some more. "Yeah, I stopped over as soon as I got home from Saturday mass, but it was all dark in the basement, and I didn't want to knock on the front door. I figured you were still asleep."

"You—you did?" I basically cannot wrap my head around the fact that I am actually standing on *Jake Ribano's* front porch. *Talking to him!* And did he say *mass*? Jake Ribano goes to *church*? A breeze catches the back of my neck, and I shiver, pulling my sweatshirt tight around me. Wait. Not my sweatshirt. Jake Ribano's sweatshirt. Oh! Does he think it's strange I'm wearing his sweatshirt? Should I give it back? I start to unzip it.

"What are you doing?" Jake asks.

"Oh, um, giving you back your hoodie," I mumble, slipping it off and passing it over. If only the floor could swallow me now.

Jake looks confused, then . . . Hold on, does he look hurt?

"You changed your mind?" he asks, and he even *sounds* hurt. What is happening right now?

"What? Changed my mind about what?" I ask.

Jake ties the sweatshirt around his waist, then leans against the doorway and studies our faces. After blinking a few times, he says, "Okay, so you guys seriously don't remember *anything* about last night?"

Veronica is clearly not as awed by Jake as I am. She picks a flower growing in a planter on the porch and begins pulling off the petals one at a time. "Duh. That's what we've been saying."

"Whoa." He scratches his cheek and then calls behind him, "Mom, I'm heading out for a little bit!" before stepping onto the porch and pulling the front door closed behind him.

"Follow me," he gestures. He leads the way to a jungle gym in his side yard and plops down on one of the swings. I breathe a sigh of relief that we're blocked from view of Anna Marie's house by a row of trees. The last thing we need is Mrs. Guerrero looking out the window and spotting us.

I know the clock is ticking on our find-the-float-and-return-it thing, but I'm pretty much mesmerized by the fact that I'm having a real live conversation with Jake Ribano. I sit down on the bottom of the slide. Paige leans against the metal support beam, and Veronica settles down on the lawn and picks a blade of grass she then holds in cupped hands up to her mouth. She lets out a whistle with it that I'm betting people three states over can hear.

"Veronica!" Paige yelps. Veronica drops the blade.

"Okay, so tell me what you do remember," Jake says, his feet trailing in the dirt as he swings gently back and forth.

He's looking at me, but I'm too tongue-tied to answer. Paige jumps in with, "We had this hypnotist at the party last night. Veronica's present to Anna Marie. We don't remember anything past her telling us to breathe deeply and relax our whole bodies. I think maybe she did something to give us amnesia. Veronica, where did you find her anyway?"

Veronica looks very smug. "Booked her through www.hypnotismrocks.com."

I sigh and turn again to Jake, who's swinging slowly back and forth. My stomach flutters and flops like there's a small gymnast practicing for the Olympics inside it. But I force the words out, avoiding his eyes. "I don't know how hypnosis works, but we're kind of freaking out."

Jake stops his swinging using his left toe. "Whoa. Well, you guys *were* acting a little crazy last night. I mean, I know I didn't know you very well before, but I kind of had the impression you aren't all wackadoodle normally. You kept talking about how you had to do epic things until you couldn't stay awake anymore. And let's just say you had some pretty outrageous ideas—even by my standards."

Paige answers, "Yeah, well, now there's a big blank in our brains from the time we closed our eyes for Madame Mesmer until the time we woke up this morning. And Anna Marie is missing and we need to find her. You're our only hope at this point. Can you help us retrace our steps?"

"Anna Marie is missing?" Jake says, jumping up from the swing. "Why didn't you start with that?"

All three of us look guilty. Why *hadn't* we started with that? Darn Jake Ribano and his distracting cuteness.

Paige holds up her hand. "To clarify, she's not missing anymore. We just don't have her. Or know where she is, technically. But we know *who* has her."

"What? Who?" Jake looks like he doesn't know how much to believe from three girls who arrived on his porch spewing crazy talk. "Are you saying she was kidnapped or something?"

He drags his fingers through his hair, which somehow only makes it look more perfect. I have to force myself to look away. *Focus, Meghan. Your best friend is being held by a psychotic marching band.* Well, maybe not psychotic, exactly, but who knows what those guys are capable of? They seem *really* attached to their Hedgie.

"Sort of," Paige says. "So, you know how we all stole that hedgehog float last night? And yes, we know about that. We don't remember doing it, but we did see a video, and we know you were with us. Well, the band kids who built the float have Anna Marie, and they said if we don't bring the hedgehog to them at the Dunkin' Donuts on Parker by ten a.m., we're not getting her back. Although, obviously, we're getting her back because it's not like they can *keep* her. But we'd kind of like to have her safe and sound before any parents need to get involved. Plus, it's Anna Marie's birthday, and who knows what horrible place they're keeping her or what they're feeding her or—"

"Stop!" Jake shouts, and his voice is edgy enough that I'm instantly reminded who we're dealing with. Jake didn't come by his reputation by whispering gently. When Paige stops speaking, his expression goes back to normal. "So now you need to bring the float to Dunkin' Donuts?"

"Yeah, so if you have any bright ideas of where we could find it in the next"—Paige pauses and consults the clock on her phone—"seventeen minutes, that would be great."

Jake grins, and I have to suck in another breath over how cute he is when he does that. I hadn't seen him do too much grinning before today.

"I can do even better!" he says.

CHAPTER FOURTEEN

A Hedgehog for a Lady

Jake doesn't wait for us to follow this time as he takes off up his driveway to the freestanding garage at the end of it. The outside walls are peeling, and the window has a crack running through the center of it. The double doors don't quite match up; the left one hangs lower than the right. Jake pulls a pen from the pocket of his corduroys, snaps off the metal tab, and sticks it into the lock.

A few seconds later it pops open. Paige and I stare at him, but Veronica says, "Cool."

Jake shrugs. "We lost the key. Been after my dad to get a new lock, but he keeps forgetting."

Sure, lock picking would *be a skill of Jake Ribano's.* I take a step back. It's a perfect reminder that Jake has a reputation, and I'm not exactly in the habit of hanging out with guys who have reputations, no matter how nice they seem or how cute their hair looks when it's rumpled or how they keep stealing glances at me and making my spine tickle in a weird way. Okay, to be fair, I'm not exactly in the habit of hanging out with any guys, but still.

Jake pries the doors open, flings them wide, and says, "Ta-da!"

Standing at attention in the front of the garage, shaking his fist at us, is one not-so-menacing-looking hedgehog on top of a rolling platform. Up close it looks a little (okay, a lot) rough. There are places where the metal frame shows through the papier-mâché, and the paint job is . . . not the best. Still, it's pretty cute. Not intimidating (or havocking) at all. But cute.

"Hedgie!" Veronica shouts, running up and throwing her arms around it. "He's so sweet!"

I smile shyly at Jake, who returns my grin with a smile of his own. Whoa. Just whoa. As he does, though, I suddenly remember something I'd managed to forget briefly.

I have one eyebrow. Jake Ribano is seeing me with *one* eyebrow!

I want to dissolve into a puddle under Hedgie's wheels. I quickly head to the back of the float to get out of sight. This is not my life. It can't be. No one is this tragic.

"How are we going to get it to the Dunkin' Donuts?" Paige asks, stepping close and pulling on the handle at the front of the float. Hedge is mounted on a small rolling platform, but he must not be all that light. She doesn't budge him so much as one inch. She steps back and places both hands on her hips.

Jake laughs, but in a friendly way.

"Same way we got it here," he says. "We walk it together. Or roll it, I guess. It won't be so bad with all of us helping, once we get it going. We did it last night."

Veronica puts her Mickey Mouse watch right up next to her face and studies it. "We have eleven minutes, peeps."

Peeps? I roll my eyes, because I know she can't see me. In fact, I'm hoping no one can back here in the shadows as I absently rub the smooth patch of skin above my eye.

Jake looks around the garage, taking in the contents. "I have an idea."

He tugs a silver-edged black skateboard covered in skull-and-crossbones decals off the wall where it hangs and flips it onto the ground. He steps on the board, bouncing a little to test it, before hopping off.

"I have two old motocross bikes in here too. If we can get one person riding along each side of the float to keep it from tipping over, we should be good."

Jake Ribano is fearless. I can't help but be impressed. Before this sleepover, I couldn't even go a whole night away from my own bed, and I can't even be *that* proud I managed to accomplish it last night because I don't even *remember doing it*! I can't imagine being as free-spirited as he is. While I'm busy listing all his pros in my head, Jake disappears farther into the garage to hunt down the bikes.

Paige stands next to Veronica.

"Doesn't sound like there are enough bikes for all three of us. How would you feel about heading back to Anna Marie's to run interference in case Mrs. Guerrero comes down?" Paige asks her.

Veronica nods, a very serious expression on her face. "That's probably a wise decision for me. I didn't pack my custom-painted Thor bike helmet, and I don't ride anywhere without it, so . . ."

"Oh, okay. Um, so our plan makes sense then." Paige avoids my eyes, and I know it's because she's afraid she'll laugh if she doesn't. Veronica is definitely one of a kind. But mostly harmless and even a little fun. In fact, odd as she is, she's starting to grow on me.

Jake wheels the bikes out, then returns with three black helmets tucked under his arms. Veronica holds her hands up and shakes her head, so he tosses one to Paige and then approaches me with the other.

"Here, let me," he says, stepping close and gently placing it on my head. I might hyperventilate. Why is he doing this for me but not for Paige? He looks me straight in the eyes (oh God, is my lack of eyebrow even worse up close?) as he fastens the buckle under my chin.

Can't. Breathe. Send. Medic.

What is going on here? Why is he being so nice to me? We've never even spoken before last night, and he usually keeps completely to himself at school. But this version of Jake Ribano is smiling and . . . and *sweet*.

I have to say it again: Of all the weird things this morning, this just might be the weirdest. And that's saying a lot, considering that a havocking hedgehog, seventeen ducklings, and a blackmailing marching band are on the same list.

Before I can really take in the moment, Jake has fastened my helmet and is stepping away, putting the third one onto his own head. Then he unties his sweatshirt and instead ties the rope attached to the front of Hedgie around his waist. He hops easily onto the skateboard and turns to look back at us.

"Catch," he says, tossing me the hoodie I'd returned to him not ten minutes ago. "Um, it's, uh, it's kind of cool out," he adds with a casual shrug. "Ready?"

"Have fun, guys!" Veronica says, waving.

I slip into the sweatshirt again and swing one leg over the seat. I've never ridden a dirt bike. It's so much shorter than my ten-speed. Will it ride differently too? The last thing I need is to wipe out in front of Jake Ribano. At least the helmet covers my missing eyebrow, but I still don't want to draw any extra attention to myself. Especially not by being a klutz. I think I might be scared.

With one foot on the ground, I raise the other pedal and set my foot in place, ready to push off. *Be brave, be brave, be brave,* I repeat in my head, but it only works slightly better at calming me than the counting I did this morning.

Still, what choice do I have, really? *Do it for Anna Marie.* That's it. That's perfect inspiration. I picture Anna Marie, waiting for us behind the Dunkin' Donuts. I bet she's biting her cuticles. She always does that when she's nervous. I imagine her face breaking out into a smile when she sees us ride up with Hedgie. Yup, that's the image I need in my head right now. Perfect.

I can't see Paige on the other side of me because of the giant hedgehog between us, so I rely on Jake for the signal. When he gives one, I quickly shove my foot down and balance on the short bike. My knees are practically at my chin, but I'm relieved it isn't *that* different from riding my own. Except that the hedgehog doesn't move at first, and I'm worried I'm going to crash into Jake's back. But Veronica must push from behind at the last second because the platform suddenly rolls over the bump between the garage and driveway, wobbles a bit, and then straightens before propelling down the driveway.

I have to pedal hard to keep up. I steal a glance behind me and spot Veronica waving as we speed into the street.

I stare hard at the asphalt as we pass Anna Marie's house, kind of like a little kid who thinks covering her own eyes means no one else can see her during hide-and-seek. But I really cannot begin to contemplate the thought that after everything we're going through, Mrs. Guerrero might be near any windows at the exact moment a giant parade float being pulled by a boy on a skateboard and guarded by two girls on BMX bikes (two girls who are supposed to be safely asleep in her basement) flies by her house.

Nothing anyone can do about it now anyway. We're going too fast to stop, and already we're making the widest turn possible onto Crestmont and pulling out of sight. In the worst-case scenario, if she *had* seen us, Veronica could come up with some kind of cover story and, once we get back—*with* Anna Maria—we can figure something out. As long as we have her, none of the rest matters.

I breathe in the wind rushing at my face and, without meaning to, I giggle. Okay, so in no universe could I ever have imagined *this* would be my morning, but now that I know we're *this close* to having Anna Marie back, safe and sound, I have to admit it's exactly the kind of fun I'd hoped to have at the sleepover. Well, maybe not *exactly* the kind of fun, but . . . fun. Real fun and real adventure. No one could argue this sleepover isn't epic. No one.

Jake glances over his shoulder at me. My stomach does something weird that I don't think has that much to do with the exhilaration of the bike ride. Before I can even form a thought or talk myself out of it, I smile at him, and he gives me a thumbs-up.

We pedal/skate hard and fast, keeping as close as possible to the side of the road to allow the very occasional car to pass. Only two do, one of them honking the entire time. We look ridiculous. I get it.

Luckily, we live in a quiet neighborhood and, because it's a weekend, it's emptier than usual around town. We have one last turn to make and then we'll see the Dunkin' Donuts. At this rate, we ought to get there exactly on time.

Of course, I forgot to take into account one minor detail: the Dunkin' Donuts is at the bottom of Hillside Avenue while we . . . are at the top. And Hillside Avenue is very, *very* appropriately named.

Jake crests the hill first and disappears over the top before I can yell to him to slow down. Is he remembering how steep the decline is? He has to be, right? My dad and I sometimes take walks on this road, and it's almost hard not to keep from jogging when we head down the top half. My stomach churns again, and this time it has nothing to do with a cute boy. I wish I could see Paige. If she's calm, maybe I can be, but if she's not . . .

The first set of the float's wheels bump over the edge of the hill. Then the second. I don't really have a choice but to follow. I mean, I can't abandon the float, or it might tip over.

Then again, if it does start tipping over, what am I possibly going to do about it? I'm already hanging on to the bike's handlebars for dear life.

I hit the hill at a pretty decent speed. As we start down, I have to take my feet off the pedals because they're spinning too fast for my legs. Where are the brakes on these types of bikes?

Up ahead, Jake is crouched low on his skateboard, speeding along, the rope tight around his waist. He seems perfectly comfortable. Maybe this will be okay after all. I start to relax, but then . . .

We hit a small bump. Hedgie rocks for a second, then recovers, then shifts sideways on the platform, sliding toward my edge. Whoaaaaaaa. I wobble on my bike, legs out, pedals spinning, and reach for the hedgehog with my right arm. My left arm is so tight on the handlebar, it might meld to the metal at any second. I push with my right arm just enough . . . to . . . there! I settle Hedgie back into place before bouncing away as I fight to get the bike balanced.

Now Hedgie jerks to the right side, overcorrecting, but staying upright on the thin piece of plywood that forms his platform. I'm pretty sure no one took into account to make it sturdy enough for downhill slalom racing when they were building it. On the other side of me I still can't see Paige, but I can hear her whooping. Leave it to Paige to be enjoying this.

A minute ago even *I*, scaredy-cat Meghan, had been grinning ear to ear at the adventure of escorting a giant hedgehog float across town, but that was before there was actual danger involved.

Now, though?

We're only halfway down the hill, and Hedgie is picking up speed. The rope between the float and Jake starts to sag. He isn't far enough ahead, and it doesn't seem like he could go any faster. Hedgie is gaining on him!

I try desperately to line up my feet with the pedals, but they're spinning around so fast, they make me dizzy. The most I can do is hold on and pray. Or scream. It's possible I've been doing a little of that, too, and I really, really, *really* hope the wind is carrying it away from Jake. There is zero need for him to think I am a wimp.

Although if Jake is thinking about anything right now, it probably has to do with the giant hedgehog nipping at his heels. I can tell he's trying to keep his own balance while using one hand to untie the rope around his waist. The one that attaches him to Hedgie. I scream again as the float goes careening past Jake, whipping him around so he's now facing up the hill. Facing *me*. Instead of pulling the hedgehog float, he's now getting dragged by it. His arms flail as he struggles to stay on the skateboard riding backward.

Without Hedgie between us anymore, I can see Paige

clearly now too. Unlike me, she's managed to keep her feet on the pedals, but they're circling around so fast, her legs must be jelly. She's not whooping anymore; she's concentrating hard on the road and white-knuckling the handlebars.

We're three-quarters of the way down the hill.

If we can just hang on for a little longer, we'll hit the spot where the road levels out, and all will be well. I think. At least Hedgie is sticking to the center of the road, and there are no cars in either direction. It could be worse.

Now we're nearly to the bottom, and I can feel the road evening out. We're going to make it!

The very second that thought forms in my head, I spot it. A giant pothole to put all other potholes to shame. And Jake can't see it because he's skating backward.

I lean low over my handlebars, trying to pick up speed, which is so, so insane, really, but what else can I do? I *have* to try to help, don't I? I'm edging closer to both Jake and the float, keeping my eyes focused on the pothole and on Hedgie. It seems like . . . yes! It definitely looks like it's going to pass right between Hedgie's wheels.

It does! By some miracle, the platform is lined up just so, and the wheels coast over clean asphalt on either side of the hole.

Hedgie is upright. Hooray! Jake gets the rope loose from his waist and detaches himself from the float. He's in the process of spinning forward again. I'm only a few feet away from him at this point and pretty transfixed by his movements as he tries to regain his balance. He's so graceful. Does that sound weird? Can guys be described as—

Thunk. My tires dip into another gaping hole I never even saw coming and slam against the front side of it. The bike stops in place. I, however, do *not* stop in place. I go soaring over the handlebars, arms out like I'm some kind of flying squirrel, and catch mega-air, landing on top of a stinking pile of black plastic trash bags someone has placed at the end of their driveway on the side of Hillside Avenue.

Paige screams.

I put my head down, not even caring how smelly it is. I face-planted into garbage! I gingerly move each limb, testing them. Man, I'm going to have one monster of a black-and-blue mark basically everywhere, but at least nothing seems broken. Even so . . . owwwwww!

Paige's bike lands with a crash next to me, and she runs over. "Oh my God, are you okay?"

I roll and squint up at her, just as Jake arrives over her shoulder. I just . . . I can't even.

"Does anything hurt?" he asks, looking worried.

I manage a snort. It might be faster to give him a list of things that *don't* hurt. But I smile to reassure him. "I'm okay," I croak.

Paige holds out a hand to help me up. I notice Jake trying

not to wrinkle his nose at the trash smell. I shake my head, roll off the pile of garbage, and struggle to my feet. My cheeks are practically burning as I brush off my clothes. Ewww. Also, ouch.

They aren't visible because of my pants, but I can tell my legs are all scraped up. Great. In addition to having one eyebrow, I'm now going to be covered in black-and-blue marks *and* Band-Aids. Supercute.

Paige grimaces and then steps close to subtly pull something from my shoulder. She quickly tosses it behind her but not fast enough. A dirty, squishy banana peel. Was on my shoulder. In front of Jake Ribano. Oh my God, seriously, universe? I stole *one* teeny, tiny (maybe not *so* tiny) hedgehog float, and this is how you punish me?

Jake turns away really fast, but not before I see him push down a laugh. Paige looks ready to lose it too. And then I surprise myself, because *I* do.

I totally let loose . . . and it feels sooo good. It's like all the adrenaline from the ride and the crash just spills out of me in the form of laughter. I did it! I did something totally crazy and so unlike myself and, sure, okay, I ended up all bruised and with garbage covering me in front of the boy I like, but I mean, I'm not seriously hurt or anything. And he's laughing *with* me, not *at* me. I can tell. I know I did crazy stuff last night, but that wasn't exactly within my control. This *was*, and I *still* said yes. And it was superscary, but also kind of awesome.

A car honks behind us, and immediately I crash back to earth. Hedgie! Where is he? We don't have time for this! Anna Marie is steps away, and we need to get her back.

"Hedgie!" I cry. "How bad is he?"

If Hedgie is ruined, will the band kids try to keep my best friend? What else do Paige and I have to bargain with? Nothing.

Jake points over my shoulder. "Look."

Even though I don't want to, I take my time turning around because *ouch*! But when I do, there's Hedgie the Hedgehog, arms outstretched in a not-so-menacing pose, sitting pretty and perfect atop his wooden platform at the base of the hill. Mocking me, almost. The car edges around him, the driver leaning out the window to yell something at us.

That just makes me giggle again. Is this what being reckless feels like? No wonder people like it.

I catch Paige's and Jake's eyes before smiling. "Let's finish this thing." I feel invincible right now.

They let me set the pace—a slow one—and Jake wheels my bike (which, thankfully, I didn't damage) for me as we catch up with the float. He ties the rope around his waist again, balancing his skateboard on his lap, and hops up on my bike to pull Hedgie the last little way to the Dunkin' Donuts parking lot. Paige gives the platform a push to get the float going and then rolls her bike alongside me as we walk the short distance.

She flashes her phone at me. One minute early. We both smile.

Jake pedals the float behind the back of the store. As soon as Paige and I round the corner a few seconds later, we spy the pack of band kids.

"Hedgie!" Flute Girl cries, racing up to us. She walks the perimeter of the float, carefully inspecting her creation.

The kid with the baton approaches too, smacking it against his palm.

"I have to give you credit. I didn't think you'd get here in time," he says.

I peer around him, trying to catch sight of Anna Marie.

"Well, we did," Paige says, her voice hard and tough sounding. "So give her to us right now!"

Baton Boy looks at Flute Girl, who is now holding the rope Jake untied from his waist. She nods. "We're good."

Flute Girl turns and signals to the boy with the too-short pants. "Bring it over."

"Hey! That's our friend. She's not an 'it'!" Paige exclaims.

"Look, I love my phone as much as the next kid, but I don't assign it a gender. To each her own, I guess. Although, technically speaking, half of all ladybugs are male, you know."

"Ladybugs? What the heck are you talking about?" Jake asks. "Where's Anna Marie?"

I have a bad feeling. A really bad, sinking feeling.

I pat my pockets, checking for my cell phone, my *Ladybug* cell phone, but my pockets are empty. My worst fear is confirmed when the boy in the flood pants tosses a small item to Jake, who catches it one-handed. Sure enough, when he turns it over in his hand, it's a small, red phone with black dots and a total of two buttons: Home and emergency. Jake studies it, total confusion on his face.

"Where's Anna Marie?" Paige screams, but now it's the band kids turn to look confused.

"Who's Anna Marie?" Flute Girl asks.

CHAPTER FIFTEEN

Moment of Truth

Paige juts out her hip and points a finger at Flute Girl. "Anna Marie! Our friend. *You* said you had her!"

The kid with the baton holds his hands out, palms up. "Look, we don't know anything about any Anna Marie. When we said we had something you'd really want, we meant your cell phone. It was lying in the parking lot in the exact spot Hedgie was stolen from. Must have fallen out of your pocket when you were trying to get the float going. Hey, if I lost mine, my dad would ground me for a month. We kind of figured your parents would too, so it was the perfect bargaining chip."

"You mean blackmailing chip," Jake says with a sneer. Suddenly he looks exactly like the tough guy I always thought he was, and I catch my breath. But he's on my side, and I'm extra-glad about that. We need Anna Marie back—whatever it takes.

"Call it what you want. We have our float; you have your phone. All's well that ends well as far as we're concerned. Now, if you'll excuse us, we need to finish decoupaging Hedgie's flower headband before showtime!"

The Hillside Heights kids surround the float and push/pull it out of the Dunkin' Donuts parking lot. We stand helplessly by the Dumpster, watching the giant hedgehog disappear from view. Jake holds up my phone, and I slink over to silently take it from him and place it into my pocket. If it is possible to be any more embarrassed today, I really can't imagine how. Even though I *thought* that was the case just a few minutes ago when I had banana dripping from my shoulder.

"I give up," I say. "Paige, we have to tell Mrs. Guerrero. Anna Marie could be in real trouble, and we're wasting valuable time." I put my head in my hands. I'm *d-o-n-e*, done.

Jake kicks at some gravel. "I think she's right. Let's head home. I can fill you in on everything *I* remember from last night, though I gotta warn you, I don't know how helpful it's gonna be."

Paige answers by dropping her shoulders, clipping her helmet buckle under her chin, and swinging a leg over her bike.

I eye my own (well, technically Jake's) bike. I *know* the old expression that you're supposed to get right back on the horse that throws you and that I had some big epiphany among the trash bags about how much fun it could be to throw caution to the wind, but the very last thing I want to do right now is ride the Bike of Death home. Plus, my knees are throbbing, and I don't want to think about how much worse pedaling will make them hurt.

Jake seems to read my mind. "I have an idea," he says before disappearing behind the Dumpster with his skateboard. He returns empty-handed.

"I can come back for that later." He hops onto the dirt bike and motions for me to place my feet on the two wide, round posts sticking out from either side of the back tire. "Jump on!"

I stare at the bike. Jake says, "It's what they're designed for. Hop on and hold tight."

Hold tight? Does he mean hold tight to him? Like, put my hands on his shoulders while he pedals?

Um, no. No, no, no, nope, no. Not gonna happen. He's a *boy*!

And I smell like a trash bag.

I stand helplessly in the parking lot, debating, when a squawk from the drive-through speaker makes me jump.

"One mocha latte with two shots of vanilla please."

"Thank you. Pull forward."

Paige's eyes widen at something behind me. "Megs, is that . . . ?"

I only know one person who is addicted to mocha lattes with two shots of vanilla. This? Can't be good.

I tuck my face as far into my bike helmet as I can manage and then put my chin next to my armpit. Turning ever so slightly, I peer around my shoulder at the drive-through window and lose my breath. I only know one person who is addicted to mocha lattes with two shots of vanilla *and* drives a hunter-green Volvo station wagon with a dent in the passenger side from the time she backed into a pump at the gas station.

My heart whomp-whomps in my ears as I lift my eyes and find my own mother staring back at me! My *mother*!

Mom's eyes narrow, and her head tilts as she squints in my direction. She reaches across the top of the dashboard for her glasses. I know from being in the car with her for a zillion of these drive-through orders that she always tosses them up there while she rummages through her wallet for cash. I am incredibly blessed right now that my mother is too vain for bifocals.

I spin back to Jake, place one foot and then the other firmly on the metal outposts, and grab on to his shoulders. I have no time to think about this. None at all. We have to get out of here before my mom gets those glasses on.

"Go!" I scream.

This is so weird. I have my hands resting on Jake Ribano's shoulders! We're safely away from Dunkin' Donuts now, cruising down a side street that I know for a fact my mom wouldn't take to get home, and I'm holding on to Jake Ribano for dear life. Yes, I am.

Okay, so my feelings about boys have changed over the last few years, and I don't honestly think they have cooties anymore (though the jury is still way out on a few of the guys in my class—like Owen Richardson), but it's not like I've ever been *this* close to one.

Much less Jake "Tough Guy" Ribano. How many times have we tried to spy on Jake from Anna Marie's bedroom? Okay, so he wasn't often outside, but we always had fun trying. Anna Marie will *die* when I tell her about this!

Anna Marie.

My stomach falls all the way into my shoes. I got so wrapped up in escaping before my mom noticed me and then on the whole hanging-on-to-Jake thing that I haven't really processed what we're about to do. How are we going to break the news to Mrs. Guerrero that we don't know where her daughter is and that we've been running around town all morning looking for her instead of confessing right away? Are we horrible people? Is there anything—*anything*—we're overlooking?

I have to know right now. I lean forward a little and speak into Jake's ear, trying not to blush as I do. "So you're going to fill us in on everything you remember when we get back?"

Jake nods and turns his head slightly to answer me. Yikes!

Wasn't expecting that. Way, way too close to Jake's face for comfort!

He seems freaked out too, because he whips his head forward pretty fast and settles for calling back to me, "I can tell you some now, if you can hear me okay?"

I nod but then realize he can't see me. Whoops. "I can hear you!" I yell.

Jake angles his face ever so slightly sideways and says, "There's not that much. I was hanging around the gym after the team's late practice last night, helping get the place ready for the game today while my dad met with the coach in his office, when you guys came in and scared me half to death. You were on a total mission to take those baby ducks. I tried to talk you out of it, but . . ."

This surprises me. Like, really, really surprises me. Jake is known for being trouble, so I figured he was the one who tried to talk us *into* some of the stuff we did last night—not out of it. Jake *is* a bad boy, *isn't he?* Except, if so, why isn't he acting anything but nice and why did he say he was at school "helping" and not "for detention" and why is he here so willingly now and why did he go to church this morning and why is he wearing corduroys instead of his trademark black hoodie?

Oh. Wait. The hoodie question I can answer.

"Then what happened?" I ask. I'm so confused.

"Okay, so then we brought the ducklings to the basement

and got them settled into the bathtub. You wanted to stay and take care of them, but Paige and Anna Marie kept talking about how there could be 'even more epic,' and you agreed pretty quickly. Anna Marie had the idea to free other duck-lings from captivity, so you guys decided to go to Hillside Heights to see if their science classes were doing the same project. I tried to reason with you, but when I saw you were gonna go either way, I figured I'd go along to make sure you all were safe."

That is . . . Well, that is really sweet. I don't know what to make of it either, so I just say, "And then?"

"And then we went to Hillside. You guys were pretend-ing you were ninjas, and sneaking up to the doors, but then we turned the corner and saw the parking lot, and Veronica completely flipped out over the hedgehog float and decided she had to have it. Which you all thought was hilarious and a great idea, by the way. You pretty much forgot about break-ing in after that, and I was so happy about it, I helped out with taking Hedgie. We rolled it back to my garage and, um, that was it."

"That was it?"

"Uh, yeah. Pretty much. I mean, uh, the rest isn't import-ant. Nothing that would help find Anna Marie, for sure."

Before I have the chance to puzzle out what he means by "the rest," we're pulling into Jake's driveway. Paige stops in front of us, enters the garage, and props her bike against the wall where it had been to start. I suddenly realize I still have my hands on Jake's shoulders, even though we've stopped moving now. I drop them like he's on fire and edge backward over the rear tire. Jake glances at me and then unbuckles his helmet. He holds out his hand for my helmet.

Great. Now, on top of the whole one eyebrow thing, he's also going to see me with helmet hair. Just perfect.

I fork it over and busy myself playing with the zipper on Jake's sweatshirt. He certainly hasn't told me how I got it last night.

One mystery at a time, Meghan.

"Let's get this over with," Paige says, and all her trademark happy-go-lucky attitude is wiped from her face. She looks like we're about to face a firing squad. Maybe we are.

Jake groans. "I should probably be there cuz she's gonna want to ask me questions anyway."

Jake Ribano is turning out to be not at all what I thought. The basement looks significantly de-Silly Stringed when we return, and the Mountain Dew cans are all in a blue plastic recycling bin by the back door. Veronica is busily scrubbing at a spot on the carpet. It looks like the same spot I stepped in on my way to the bathroom this morning. I make a face.

"What *was* that?" I ask.

Veronica shrugs. "Search me. Some kind of green goo.

Didn't taste like anything I'd ever had before." She peers over my shoulder. "Where's Anna Marie?"

Paige doesn't answer, throwing herself onto the couch and raising a hand to her forehead. Veronica looks between me and Jake, and we quickly fill her in.

"Oh man" is all she has to say. Then: "I guess it's a good thing I cleaned up a little. Maybe it will earn us a few brownie points when we tell Anna Marie's mom we've lost her kid."

Jake grimaces. "I'm pretty sure when she finds out we waited hours to tell her about her missing daughter, she won't care one bit if a bomb went off in the basement."

I put a hand on Veronica's shoulder. "But it really does look much better. You did a great job."

Veronica puffs out her chest and smiles. It's almost like no one has ever complimented her before.

"So, we're gonna do this?" I ask.

Paige looks at Veronica, and Veronica looks at Jake, who answers, "We'll just tell her the truth. As of two o'clock in the morning, Anna Marie was safely back home, and she and Veronica and Paige were brushing their teeth and getting ready for bed."

It takes me a second, but then I snap to attention. "And me, right? I was too, wasn't I?"

Jake studies his feet. "Well, uh . . . not exactly. You, um . . . you stayed outside on the picnic bench with me. To talk."

My jaw drops. "I *did*?" I'd stayed up waaaaaay late into the night chatting with *Jake Ribano*? *By myself*? Was that before or after I went singular on the eyebrow?

Jake mumbles, "Yeah."

Suddenly I wish—really, really wish—there was time to find out more about this mysterious talk. But there isn't. We have to tell Mrs. Guerrero. We girls join hands and take a deep breath.

"Now or never. We can do this," Paige says.

We squeeze once, then drop hands and follow Jake up the basement steps.

CHAPTER SIXTEEN

The YouTube Stylings of Madame Mesmer

Two minutes later we're back in the basement.

"I can't believe her mother's not home!" Paige says, and her tone makes it obvious she's super-annoyed.

The house had been extra quiet when we stepped into the hallway. We explored the downstairs, ending in the kitchen, where a scribbled message on I HEART NEW YORK notepaper read *Good morning, sleepyheads! I'll be back in an hour. Grabbing the cake for the family birthday celebration tonight. When I get home, we'll do breakfast!*

The note takes away all our resolve and courage, and we practically slump downstairs. There's nothing to do now but wait.

We all plop down on the giant sectional, except for Veronica, who snags a spot lying down on the floor. She puts her feet on the couch. "Can I just say something? It might sound weird."

Paige and I exchange yet another look—maybe our thousandth since Veronica arrived last night. Does she ever say anything that *isn't* weird?

"Sure," I answer.

"Except for the whole losing AM part," Veronica whispers, "last night was the most fun I ever had."

I straighten up and stare at her. "Wait, so you remember last night now?"

Veronica looks confused. "No!"

I squint. "But you just said it was the most fun you ever had. How do you know that if—"

"I know in my heart it must have been. We were all together. You guys are, like, my very best friends now."

I feel terrible. Veronica is weird, for sure, but also mostly sweet. Except, how could she think I'm her best friend when I don't even know her last name? But before I can find the exact right thing to say, Paige surprises the heck out of me by saying, "You're pretty cool, V. There's never a dull moment when you're around."

Veronica's smile could power the annual Hillside Carnival, and I can't help but smile too.

"Welp, let's finish cleaning," she says, as if we all didn't just totally have "a moment."

Yup, she's sweet . . . but most definitely strange.

And also right. I stand up and take the sticky pizza box out to the trash can on the back porch. Veronica offers to scrub the duckling poop from the bottom of the bathtub and, obviously, none of us are going to fight her for *that* job. Paige picks each individual M&M from the carpet while I concentrate on the Doritos bits.

Jake doesn't seem all that eager to clean (who could blame him?), but he finds his own way to help. "I'm gonna research hypnosis. Maybe if we find out more about how it works, we can figure out how to get your memory back and you might remember something helpful."

As we scrub and pick, Jake pulls out his phone and reads us facts.

"Hypnotists can't make you do anything you don't want to. You're just more susceptible to suggestions."

"Yeah, Madame Mesmer told us that," I reply.

"Do you know it stems from ancient rituals of the Orient?"

"Do *you* know that's not at all helpful to our current situation?" Paige answers, grinning to soften her sarcasm.

"I knew that," calls Veronica from the bathroom.

We work in silence for a few minutes, until Jake speaks again. "I found something. There's a Wikipedia page on posthypnotic amnesia. Here's what it says: 'Posthypnotic amnesia is the inability to recall events that took place while under hypnosis. This can be achieved by giving individuals a suggestion during hypnosis to forget what they have learned before or during hypnosis. Memories may return when these individuals are presented with a prearranged cue.'"

I stop picking up Doritos crumbs and poke at the small pile of them in my hand while I try to rearrange those sentences into regular words I can understand. "So, Madame Mesmer could have done this on purpose? Told us not to remember anything we did under hypnosis until someone says the right word to snap us out of it?"

Jake nods. "Kind of seems like that, yeah."

Veronica appears in the bathroom door to gape along with Paige and me. "But why would she have done that? *Why?* That's so . . . so mean!"

"No offense, Veronica, but you did find her on the Internet. She might not be *that* reputable," I say, giving her a sympathetic look.

"Okay, so we just need to call her and find out what the cue is. What's the website?" Jake asks. Veronica tells him, and he bends over his phone for a few minutes, staring at his screen. "Got a customer service number!" he finally says.

Jake presses send on the call.

He's quiet for a bit, and I'm just starting to worry that no one will be there on a Saturday morning, when Jake speaks.

"Hello? Um, hi. We had a party last night and one of your hypnotists came and put my friends under and now they can't remember anything that happened between then and this morning. We need to know the cue to snap them out of it. . . . Uh-huh . . . No . . . Yes . . . No . . ."

"What are they saying?" asks Paige, pulling on Jake's sleeve. He swats her away and holds a finger to his lips.

"Yes, okay. Hold on."

He asks us, "What was the name of the woman again?"

"Madame Mesmer," we all blurt at once.

Jake repeats into his phone. "Madame Mesmer."

He holds it away from him to peer at the handset and then hits a button. The phone switches to speakerphone, and easy listening music plays into the basement. "I'm on hold," he whispers.

None of us say a word as we wait, but I pick at a loose thread on my shirt and make promises to the universe about all the good deeds I'll do if we can figure this out and find Anna Marie.

Finally there's a click. "Hello?"

"Yeah, we're here," Jake says.

"Okay, thank you for holding. I reached Madame Mesmer and, as I suspected, she said she would never in a million years have instructed you to forget the night. It is regrettable that she did not bring you out of the hypnosis herself and she will be on probation for that offense, but she says she did give you very clear instructions that you were to snap out of the hypnosis as soon as you heard the words

New York. She says she called two hours after she left and spoke the words into the phone when one of you answered. Someone named Paige. She gave clear instructions for this Paige person to repeat it to the remainder of the guests and got assurances it would be done. I'm sorry, but there is no other cue or trigger word."

Paige shakes her head back and forth wildly. "That's a lie! I never talked to her. I don't remember answering the phone last night!"

I give her a look. Paige could have easily answered a phone without recalling it. But then why was she still affected by the hypnosis? Even if she'd somehow forgotten to relay the message to us if she heard the trigger words, wouldn't *she* have a clear memory of everything that happened? Although Paige was desperate to have a crazy night to prove something to her brother and sister, and, probably just as much for my benefit too, if I'm being honest. And okay, maybe—*maybe*—she would have kept the charade up so we could do some crazy stuff last night, but she would *never, ever* keep it going for so long. Especially not with Anna Marie missing. Paige is just as worried about her as I am.

Jake puts his face right next to the phone. "Wait. So are you saying Madame Mesmer just left them when they were still under hypnosis? Who does that?" He's practically growling, and I can see how he comes by his reputation when he gets like this. Still, it's kind of sweet that he's getting all protective of us.

There is a ton of throat clearing on the other end of the phone. "Yes, well, sir, that is certainly very much against company guidelines, and we will be taking disciplinary actions against Brittany, er, Madame Mesmer. I'm so sorry for any inconvenience. Perhaps I can make up for it with a twenty-dollar-off coupon for the next party you book with us."

Paige snorts and grabs the phone. "Are you insane? Our friend is missing, and if anything happens to her, my father is going to sue you into oblivion. You better start getting moving supplies good and ready because—" She holds the phone away from her.

"I think he hung up on me!" The phone droops in her hand as she turns to us, and I can't be sure, but I think I see tears prickling in her eyes.

There's no way Paige is lying about not getting the call last night. I've never seen laid-back Paige so worked up over *anything*. Not even the time her sister tried to convince her she was adopted, with a fake birth certificate and everything.

From the staircase we hear giggling.

Paige's voice is like ice. "Max?" she calls, and her tears are gone just like that. "Get your butt down here, you brat!"

"Is it time for my kiss?" comes his reply.

Jake shoots me a questioning glance, and I roll my eyes and shake my head. "Don't even ask."

A second later Max appears with a video camera pressed to his eye.

"May I help you ladies?" He seems less confident when he turns to Jake. "W'sup, dude?"

"Little man," Jake answers with a nod.

"Did you just get back? Does this mean your mom's home?" Paige asks, hand on hip.

"Nope. Mom left me here with you guys. Said to wake you if I needed anything. Don't worry. I didn't spill the beans that you were already up. Or that you weren't even home when she left. Couldn't waste my chance to get the house all to myself." He practically cackles. "So do you, like, seriously not know where my sister is? Major bummer."

He smirks, and I bop him on the head. "You could try acting more concerned."

"Think I'll get her room now?" he asks, making a break for the stairs before I can hit him again.

After the door at the top of the stairs slams, Jake says, "Sorry, guys. I thought we'd get something more out of that call or—"

"Hold on a second! Does Anna Marie have a laptop I can borrow?" Veronica asks.

"You can use my phone," Jake offers.

"Need a bigger screen," Veronica replies. What is she up to?

Paige gestures to the bar. "I think it's over there. What are you thinking?" she asks, but Veronica just grabs the computer, plops down on her cot, and holds up a hand as she begins typing. "It's a hunch. Give me a few minutes."

Paige and I have basically nothing else to do but to go back to cleaning. Jake tries to do more research on his phone, although I don't know what else he thinks he's gonna find. I guess he just doesn't want to scrub mysterious green goo, and I don't blame him one bit. At least the basement is practically sparkling twenty minutes later when Veronica whistles.

"Eureka!" she says. "Trust me, you guys are gonna wannna see this!"

We rush to the corner of the basement where Veronica sits on her cot, Anna Marie's laptop on her knees.

She's pointing at a screen open to a YouTube channel. It's playing the same video the marching band kids had shown us earlier. On-screen, Hedgie picks up speed and begins rolling faster as Anna Marie and I giggle uncontrollably. I get an instant lump in my throat. Oh, Anna Marie, where *are* you?

"We already saw this," Paige says.

"I know," Veronica answers. "But we never stopped to think about who filmed that video. Or who put it on YouTube. When I saw Max's video camera, it got me thinking."

"You think *Max* followed us and filmed us?" Paige asks, clearly stunned.

But I'm not. Not shocked at all, actually. It makes so much sense, I'm annoyed I didn't think of it first.

"Why not?" I ask. "He's been trying to film us ever since we got here last night. Who's to say he didn't sneak out behind us?"

Jake's eyes narrow. "That's a good point. The kid is always looking for trouble."

I bite down on my lip because isn't that like the pot calling the kettle black? Although, maybe not. Once again I realize that the Jake Ribano I just spent half the morning with doesn't match the image I had of him at all. Is it somehow possible that I (and everyone else) have been so, so wrong about him? But then, why had he let us all think he was one way when he clearly isn't? It doesn't make any sense.

Veronica clicks off the video and points the screen's arrow at the YouTube icon. "Check out the channel name."

"Max-a-Million," says Paige, leaning over Veronica's shoulder. "That little *brat*!"

"That's not all," says Veronica. She scrolls past a whole bunch of videos whose titles start with "Minecraft Mod" until she hits on the most recent updates. The video we just watched was called "Havocking Hedgehog Unleashed," and just a bit farther down is one titled "Madame Mesmer's Mystical Masterpiece."

Veronica's hand hovers over the track pad.

"Click it," I order. My voice has a weird tone to it, and I

have a matching weird feeling in my belly. I both want to see what's on that video . . . and don't. But . . .

"We need to see," I say.

"Okay," says Veronica. "Here goes nothing."

Veronica expands the video to full screen, and there's the basement as it looked pre-Silly String explosion/Mountain Dew tower/crunched M&M's. Our sleeping bags were still rolled up tight, and Anna Marie was standing casually next to the rest of us as we listened to Madame Mesmer say:

"You will feel very relaxed and you will lose all inhibitions. You will be steered by your subconscious, the part of you that controls your actions in the background so subtly, you aren't aware of it. For example, when you breathe in and out, you aren't aware of every breath. That action is controlled by your subconscious. But under hypnosis, your subconscious will drive your actions. You won't feel the need to weigh and measure every act. You will just go with everything."

The on-screen Veronica can't stop giggling, and the camera captures Anna Marie elbowing her and saying, "Shh . . ."

It's so good to see Anna Marie, even if it's only on a laptop screen. She has to be okay. She just *has* to be.

I watch Madame Mesmer instruct us to lie down and imagine ourselves in our happy places. It's weird to see myself on camera. It's even more awkward to know Jake Ribano is standing right next to me watching too. I feel vulnerable. I must look so stupid lying there, pretending to be in the art room at school. I steal a glance at him, but his face doesn't have any expression other than maybe curiosity.

Watch the video, Meghan. Clues, remember? Look for clues.

I turn my attention back to the screen, where Madame Mesmer is saying:

"Next, I want you to imagine yourself flying through the air. . . . Take a rest on a puffy cloud and then swoosh back through the air again."

Oh God, this was before I was under hypnosis, so I remember this part. I definitely swooped my arms. Sure enough, there I am on-screen, doing some sort of weird flying-while-lying-down arm movements. I glance at Jake again, and his cheek is caved in a little, like he might be biting it to keep from laughing. At least the other girls are making flying motions too. We do look pretty ridiculous. Madame Mesmer counts to ten slowly and says:

"You are now in a state of hypnosis. You are safe. Your entire body feels relaxed and free. You are peaceful as you sink into a deeper and deeper state of hypnosis. You are safe. You are free."

Ha! I'm safe, at least, but I am feeling pretty far from peaceful.

Especially since that moment marks the final thing I remember from last night . . . and there's still plenty of time left in this video.

CHAPTER SEVENTEEN

Madame Mesmer's Mystical Masterpiece

Over my shoulder, Jake snorts. "I'm sorry, but it sounds so hokey. And look at you guys. It's like you're about to fall asleep. Some party entertainment!"

Veronica and I turn and say, "Shh!" at the same time. Jake pretends to zip his lips and throw away the key while rolling his eyes. We return our attention to the screen, and dread prickles the back of my neck because Madame Mesmer is pointing to me! I definitely don't remember this. Please, please, please don't let me have done anything embarrassing. I glance at Jake again. Oh please.

Madame Mesmer points to me.

"What's your name?"

"Meghan."

"Okay, Meghan. Let's see how you're responding to the hypnosis. When you hear the words *Magnificent Madame Mesmer*, you are going to jump up and down on one foot."

She strolls back and forth across the basement carpet. She seems like she's in full-on performer mode, looking out over a nonexistent audience and waiting a beat before whispering, "Magnificent Madame Mesmer."

Aaaaaaand there I go. I jump up, grab my left ankle, and pull it against my thigh before bouncing up and down on my right foot. The whole time I have this goofy grin on my face.

Jake laughs. "That's so awesome! I have to learn this skill!"

Paige punches him on the arm. "Just what we need. You with mind-control powers."

I basically want to melt into the carpet. Jake Ribano is watching me jump on one foot. Seriously. Is there anything more embarrassing? Well, yes, obviously. I did land in a pile of garbage an hour ago. And at least I have two eyebrows in the video, but still. How much humiliation can one person handle in a single morning? And the worst part of it is, who knows what's coming next? I contemplate putting my fingers over my eyes before watching the rest of the video. On-screen I begin to lose my breath from all the jumping in place. Madame Mesmer notices and says: "Oh sorry. That's all. You can stop now."

Immediately, I drop my ankle and stand perfectly still. Paige, Anna Marie, and Veronica are all smiles, but it doesn't seem like they're laughing at me so much as just having fun in general.

"Okay, let's try this with the rest of you. Come to a seated position. When you hear a ringing noise, you are going to answer your shoe. On the other end of the phone will be the person you most want to speak with. Ready? *Brrrrng.*"

Oh man. All four of us slip off our shoes and say hello into them. Madame Mesmer points to Paige.

"What's your name, sweetie?"

"Paige."

"Perfect. Paige, who is on the phone with you right now?"

"Taylor Swift!"

In the video, Paige screams and clutches her phone to her chest. Okay, that's actually pretty funny. I dart a look at Paige and see her laughing at her screen self.

Jake snorts.

"What?" Paige asks. "I have important questions for Swifty. Like, how does she get her red lipstick to stay on so perfectly? Mine always smudges."

Veronica pauses the video. "I've heard Vaseline. If you use a Q-tip and line your outer lip with Vaseline, it forms a border the lipstick won't bleed past."

Wait, what? Veronica, of all people, is dispensing makeup advice?

But Paige just nods. "That actually makes sense."

Veronica nods too and whispers, "Science." She hits play on the video once again.

"And what is Taylor saying to you?" Madame Mesmer asks.

"OMG! She says she wants to sing with me. She wants to do a duet at her next concert!"

"That's wonderful, dear."

"And you? Whom are you speaking with?"

I have a horrible thought the very instant Madame Mesmer turns to me. I can't be sure about my subconscious, but I know exactly who my conscious would have chosen to get a phone call from, and that is a big problem. A *very* big problem, considering he's sitting right next to me at this exact second. I blush and avoid looking at Jake. Basically, I've been trying to avoid looking at Jake ever since Veronica pushed play on this train wreck, but now I'm doing it with two bright red spots on my cheeks. This could be catastrophic.

Please say Taylor, too. Please say Taylor, too.

But I can tell by the dreamy look at my face in the video that I am not chatting with Tay Tay.

"Jaaaaaa-ke."

Oh God. Oh God, oh God, oh God. My voice was even all singsongy. This is not happening. I can't look, but I hear Jake cough and shuffle his feet.

This. Is. Not. Happening.

"How lovely," Madame Mesmer says.

Madame Mesmer moves on to Anna Marie. I let out my

breath, but I still refuse to bring my eyes anywhere near the same zip code as Jake's. Maybe ever again. He won't think that's weird at all, right?

"Anna Marie, who are you speaking with?"

The sound of Anna Marie answering, "My dad," makes me push aside my own (horrible, horrible) woes because there is my friend. Happy and healthy and right in front of us. She looks so ordinary, like she will never be anywhere but right there next to us. Not gone who knows where only a few short hours later.

Except, she's not exactly happy on-screen. In fact, she has a tear running down her cheek. I lean in closer to the laptop. Why is she crying? Madame Mesmer asks her the same thing.

"Things kind of stink with me and my dad right now," Anna Marie answers.

Madame Messmer swallows and then says, "Okay, listen to me, Anna Marie. When I next snap my fingers, you are going to feel all your guilt and anger evaporate. You will be happy again and you will be speaking to . . . to . . ."

She pauses and looks around the room, clearly grasping for a name. Her eyes settle on the poster of Great Britain above the bar in the corner.

"You will be speaking to . . . Harry Potter!"

Madame Mesmer snaps.

Immediately Anna Marie's expression lightens, and she

starts murmuring intently into the phone. Something about Horcruxes.

Veronica is up next, and Madame Mesmer moves in front of her and asks who she is talking to. Oh, this should be good. Who would Veronica most like to talk to? I can't begin to guess.

Veronica puts her finger up and continues chatting into her bear paw slipper. After a second she says, "Okay. Hold on."

"Whom are you talking to?" Madame Mesmer repeats.

Veronica's face lights up. "Oh, I'm speaking to the squirrel who lives in the tree outside my house. This is amazing."

Madame Mesmer's eyebrows shoot to the sky.

Jake's do too. Probably. I still refuse to look at him, but I can hear it in his voice when he asks, "In the realm of all the possible phone calls to get from anyone in the entire world, you chose to hear from the squirrel outside your window?"

Veronica shrugs. "Well, yeah. Squiggles is the best."

Back on-screen a snippet of "Girls Just Want to Have Fun" rings out, and Madame Mesmer dives for her bag. She fishes out a cell phone, stealing a glance back at us chatting away on our own "phones" before answering.

"What? Really? But I'd have to leave now. Yes, but I'm in the middle of— No, of course I want to meet him. You've been trying to set us up for months. Oh, I forgot. When does he go back? Okay. Okay. So it's now or never, I get it. I don't know how, but let me see if I can figure something out here.

I'll call you back when I'm on my way. Order a drink for me. I'm coming!"

Madame Mesmer stuffs her cell back into her purse and glances around the room, clearly calculating something in her head. This is why she ditched us while we were still hypnotized? For a blind date? Seriously?

"Okay, girls. Say good-bye to the person, or, erm, animal, on the other end of the phone and hang up, please. Now, we have about twenty minutes left in this party. Except I'm going to give you a bonus so we can do something really special. I have to get going, but that doesn't mean this part of the show has to end at all. Here's how it's going to work: I want you girls to have fun like you've never had fun before, until you can't stay awake anymore! When I say *party down*, you girls are going to do all the best sleepover activities you can think of. You are going to have the best time ever. And in a little while, I'm going to call you. When you hear my voice on the phone, I'm going to say, um . . . 'New York.' Those are your trigger words, and when you hear them, you will snap out of your hypnosis instantly. Does that sound like a good plan?"

We all nod.

"Whose phone would you like me to call?"

Paige raises her hand and recites her number at Madame Mesmer's prompting.

"Got it. Okay, are we ready for some fun, girls?"

Again, four nods, and Madame Mesmer gathers up her belongings and collects the scarves she'd draped over the lampshades.

"Okay, then . . . party down!"

As she heads for the basement stairs, the camera swings away from her and shakily captures the basement steps as the person recording runs up them.

No need to guess who that was.

"I'm gonna kill Madame Mesmer," Paige says, as the video ends and the screen goes black.

"Not if I get to her first," I murmur. I am scarred for life over that fake phone call to Jake. For life. Not to mention all the rest of the chaos the whole hypnosis thing caused. Anna Marie missing, obviously. But all the other crazy things we did last night too. Just . . . everything.

Jake frowns and drums his fingers on his leg. "This doesn't really explain the amnesia, though. If she did call and say, 'New York,' which makes sense since it doesn't seem like you're under hypnosis now or you'd still be partying instead of trying to find Anna Marie, you'd have your memories of the whole night, right? She didn't make any mention of not remembering things. So I don't get it."

We're all quiet for a second, considering. He's right. Ever since waking up this morning, I've felt and acted like my regular self. Well, no. That's not true. My regular self would never run through the boys' locker room or sneak into my school when it wasn't open. My regular self would never be part of a blackmailing scheme or escort a hedgehog float through town or ride behind Jake Ribano on a dirt bike. Definitely, definitely not. But I have to say, I didn't feel like I was under any influence when I chose to do those things. It just felt like I did what needed to be done in the moment to get our friend back safely. And I would do all those things again. Even if regular Meghan wouldn't.

Or maybe . . . maybe, this is regular Meghan. Just a new kind of regular.

Everyone else is quiet, trying to figure out the hypnosis stuff, but I'm quietly trying to figure out the Meghan stuff. Is this a new me? I've always been so good and followed every rule my parents or school or anyone else laid out, but maybe there's a whole other side of me that's a little bit of a rebel. Not like a lawbreaker or anything (float stealing aside!) but maybe someone who doesn't sit back and accept everything exactly as instructed. Maybe someone who lets loose and takes chances and has a little more fun. This is a lot to think about.

Paige scrolls through her cell phone and speaks into the silence. "I definitely don't remember any phone call. I remember everything from the moment I woke up, but no phone call. Although, this is superweird." She holds up her phone.

"My whole call history has been erased. Why would I have done that?"

She scrunches up her face and shakes her head. Then she adds, "Do you think the hypnosis could have just worn off from sleep?"

Jake considers. I steal tiny glances at him (okay, fine, so I can't exactly go an entire lifetime without looking at him. Or an entire morning, apparently) until he says, "I don't think so. Not with what I read anyway. What happened when you woke up? Tell me everything you do remember."

I stare off into space, trying to re-create my morning. I woke up. No, I was woken up! "I remember rolling over the remote," I say to Paige.

Paige nods. "Yeah, I remember that too. I woke up when the TV switched on. It was still connected to the Xbox from when we played Summer Dance Party last night and the music was superloud and—"

"What song?" Jake interrupts.

Paige swishes her lips side to side, straining to remember. But I already do.

"'American Boy.' My mom doesn't let me listen to hip-hop, and I hadn't heard it before last night. It's really catchy."

"True dat," adds Veronica.

Should I have just told Jake I'm not allowed to listen to hip-hop music? Will he think I'm a total baby?

He doesn't seem to have an opinion either way. He just locates the remote and switches on the TV. The game screen appears immediately, and a voice belts out: *"Take me on a trip. I'd like to go someday. Take me to New York. I'd like to see LA."*

"New York," Paige and I say breathlessly in unison.

"New York," Jake states. "That's what snapped you out of it. At least that's one mystery solved."

Paige high-fives Jake, but Veronica isn't paying attention to the TV . . . or to us at all. She's still scrolling through Max-a-Million's YouTube page.

"Maybe this will solve another," she says, pointing at the screen.

CHAPTER EIGHTEEN

When He's Bad, He's Better

"Adventures in Hypnosis" reads the name of the video. According to the time stamp, the video was posted at nine a.m. Just a few hours ago.

We all exchange looks. Veronica's mouse hovers over the play arrow. With a click, she starts the recording.

It shows Max sitting at the desk in his room, wearing a bright green I'M WITH STUPID sweatshirt with an arrow that points straight up at his chin. He's got that right. Behind him, hanging shelves are filled with odd Lego creations like a T. rex whose bottom half is the *Millennium Falcon*.

Max's eyes are full of wickedness as he introduces himself to his viewing audience. Ugh. Just . . . ugh.

"Welcome to Max-a-Million's, where the pranking is good. I'm your host, Max, and my motto is 'When I'm bad, I'm better!' Let's see what fun we have for today's episode. Many of you know my sister, Anna Marie, from previous episodes."

The screen cuts to Anna Marie wearing a bathrobe and sporting a giant towel wrapped around her hair, obviously just out of a shower. She's leaning into a mirror to apply zit cream. She's going to go mental when she sees this. *If* she sees this. No, *when* she sees this. *Stay positive, Meghan.*

On-screen, Anna Marie screams when she spots the video camera in the reflection. The next shot shows Anna Marie intently playing an air guitar in her room. This time she never even notices the camera because her eyes are closed the whole time. The last clip is Anna Marie's notebook, which has doodle after doodle of *I love Graham Cabot*.

Paige sighs. "Who can blame her? Did you guys see *Triton*? He was so hot in that movie."

I feel a little (a *lot*) weird about agreeing in front of Jake (even though I do agree, of course). I make some noncommittal sound in my throat and concentrate on the video instead.

The camera cuts back to a wildly grinning Max. He lifts one eyebrow, and his smile widens. "Yup. She's a source of endless material. If you've been following my channel, you've seen my previous videos from Anna Marie's epic birthday sleepover. We've introduced you to the cast of characters: Meghan, Paige, and the classic Veronica. We've watched them fall under the spell of hypnosis. We've watched their wild and crazy adventures as they've stolen everything from baby ducks to giant hedgehogs. And here's the very best part: They don't remember any of it! Any of it, people!"

Max rocks back in his chair and laces his fingers behind his head, elbows wide. He continues to grin at the camera. Then he winks. Rocking forward again, he props his arms on the desk and leans close to the camera.

"Wanna know why?"

Veronica hits pause on the video. I gasp as Paige's fingernails dig into my arm. Jake says a curse word and then immediately says, "Oh. Sorry."

I can't believe I can find a voice to talk to him after the embarrassment of basically revealing my crush right in front of him, but I manage. "It's okay. I'm pretty sure we're all thinking the same word in our heads."

"Death is not a kind enough punishment for that little dude. . . . ," Paige says.

I turn back to the computer. "Let's see what we're killing him for first." At my nod, Veronica hits play again.

Max's disembodied voice says, "Roll the tape," and the scene cuts to a spliced-in video, this time of Max, sitting at his desk, wearing a black T-shirt that reads, IT'S MY JOB TO BE ANNOYING, and then pulling a cell phone with a silver glitter case from his pocket and answering in a high-pitched voice. The camera is being held by someone else. Only an arm is visible, but the sleeve matches the shirt Max's friend had on last night.

"That's my *phone*!" Paige screeches, but we all shush her.

"Oh, halloo, Madame Mesmer! Yes, this is Paige. Yes, we did have so much fun tonight. What? New York? Ooooooh, *New York*. Oh wow. I . . . I feel wide-awake now. That was . . . That was crazy. But in a good way. What? Oh yes, yes, of course I'll say, *New York* to the other girls. Thank you again for coming to our party. We had a great time. Okay. G'night!"

Max cackles as he ends the call and addresses his audience.

"And that is how mayhem begins. Now for stage two. Because Sammy and I have been doing some Internet research on hypnosis, we have something a little more fun in mind for the girls downstairs. Follow us."

Max gestures to the camera. Sammy sets it on the desk next to the computer and aims at the screen where editing software is open.

"Observe," Max orders. He runs the video he'd taken in the basement of Madame Mesmer hypnotizing us, hitting record on the screen anytime she speaks. He closes out the video portion and concentrates on the audio recording he just made. From Madame Mesmer's instruction to have fun "until you can't stay awake anymore," Max isolates the word "until." From her reassurance, "I want you to remember that" he gets "remember."

When he's finally done, he has a very convincing clip of Madame Mesmer's voice saying the words, "Okay, girls! One more thing I forgot. I want you girls to have fun like you've never had fun before, but even when you snap out of your hypnosis, I don't want you to remember any of what happened until you hear the next trigger words. You will forget everything until you hear the words *Las Vegas*. That's all. Have fun!"

In a few places the editing isn't perfect—there are short gaps between the words, and it's clearly Max's disguised voice saying *Las Vegas*—but for the most part, it sounds a lot like the hypnotist herself is giving the instructions.

Jake's mouth is hanging open. "Max is diabolical," he says, and there's something that sounds just a little bit like respect, or at the very least awe, in his voice.

But I barely notice. My head is spinning in a thousand directions at once. The second I heard the words *Las Vegas* on the video, my mind exploded with hundreds of memories from the night before. I remember scooping up the baby ducklings in Miss Shanley's classroom and tucking them into the hood of Jake's sweatshirt, which he gave to me for that express purpose. That's why I had his sweatshirt! I remember tripping in the pitch black and sliding into the dewy grass outside Hillside Heights when we snuck over to "liberate" their ducks. I remember Anna Marie offering me her hand and helping me up, and I remember the two of us giggling our heads off as we pushed Hedgie the Havocking Hedgehog through our neighborhood to Jake's garage. Jake! I remember hanging out with Jake last night after everyone else had gone to bed. Oh! I remember now.

"I remember!" Veronica says, and she sounds as awe-struck as I feel.

"Me too!" Paige says, looking to me for confirmation. I nod at them both and steal a peek at Jake, whose eyes are locked on my face. He smiles.

It only takes about a minute before we lose momentum and flop back onto Veronica's cot to process everything. I feel kind of dazed.

Paige giggles. "Everything's rushing back at once. Oh whoa. We prank called Miss Shanley asking for ransom on the ducklings!"

I clap a hand over my mouth to stop my horrified laugh. "We so totally did! Do you think she'll remember? Or, wow, do you think she can trace the phone number?"

Paige considers for a second and then says, "Nah, we used Anna Marie's cell. I'm sure the school only has home numbers and parents' cells in their records."

Well, thank God for small miracles. At least we couldn't have called anywhere on my Ladybug phone. Other than my mother, of course, and I'm extremely relieved that my new-found memories don't include any suicide missions of that nature.

Jake stands behind the cot, tapping his legs again. "Um,

guys, not to interrupt the party or anything, but does any of this remembering clue you in to Anna Marie's whereabouts? You know, since she's still missing and all."

I study my lap, ashamed we were laughing and joking about prank calls at a time like this. Paige blows her hair out of her face, and Veronica shrugs sadly. Finally I whisper, "I got nothing." The other two shake their heads also, and the four of us are silent for a long moment, while I stroke absently at the spot where my eyebrow used to reside. I gasp.

"Oh my God! I did this to *myself*! I remember now. We were playing Truth or Dare. . . ."

Paige's lip goes up in one corner. "And you chose truth but then refused to answer."

Jake looks interested. "What was so secret you'd rather shave off on entire eyebrow before answering?"

I lunge across the couch at Paige, clamping my hand over her mouth before she can answer that. Now that I remember everything, I know exactly the truth I was protecting. Unfortunately, I'm not within arm's reach of Veronica.

"All she had to do was tell us was her most secret daydream."

I'm pretty sure I'm stoplight red. Jake looks equal parts embarrassed and sick to his stomach because, obviously, he can guess that one by now. He murmurs, "Oh."

Veronica shakes her head. "I don't get what the big deal is. We can all figure out it's—"

CHAPTER NINETEEN

Swings and Pinkies

But this time I'm faster. I stand up the very second Veronica's mouth opens, and I practically tackle her to the ground before she can finish her sentence.

"A kiss from Jkkkkkk," comes the muffled word as she rolls out from under me. I squeak and bury my face in the carpet. I mean, I'm sure he guessed that already, but there's thinking it, and then there's knowing it. Thanks a lot, Veronica.

Paige, good friend that she is, tries to create a distraction by saying, "Does anyone have paper and pen? I think we should make a list of everything we remember from last night. Maybe we'll find some clue that will lead to Anna Marie."

Veronica bounces back up and grabs a pen from her camping table next to the cot. She pushes her sleeve up and aims the pen at her arm. "I can write it. I took a stenography course at summer camp."

Jake is still studying his shoes. I roll over and rise to a seated position, crossing my legs and practicing deep-breathing techniques as subtly as I can. It doesn't matter if my social life will be over after my mom finds out about last night, because I will be too busy dying of humiliation to care. I almost wish my mother would show up now instead of forty-five minutes from now when she's supposed to pick me up.

I'm avoiding looking at Jake (yet again), but I can't help glancing up when he clears his throat. I bring my eyes up to his face and find him staring straight at me! He jerks his head in the direction of the basement door, raising his eyebrows in question. Wait, is he . . . Does he want me to go outside with him? Outside, like last night. I remember sitting at the picnic table with Jake, after everyone else had gone to bed. When Anna Marie had gone to bed. She'd been safe and sound and tucked into a sleeping bag.

And I'd been outside. With Jake Ribano. Alone.

Slowly, very slowly, I nod and get up from the couch. Paige glances at me and wiggles her eyebrows when I brush past her to weave behind the sofa next to Jake. I ignore her. I murmur, "We'll be right back," and follow Jake out the door. I don't dare glance behind me to see the expressions on Veronica's and Paige's faces.

Anna Marie's basement opens onto a cement patio shaded by a large deck above it. Four thick ropes are bolted to the underneath part of the deck, and they're used to hang a porch swing. Jake heads directly to it. He holds it steady and motions with a nod for me to hop on. When I've pushed myself against the back, letting my legs dangle above the ground, he sits down too. He sits right next to me. His leg brushes mine and makes me shiver just a little. I flash back to the image of him securing the bike helmet around my chin, and shiver again.

"Are you cold?" he asks. "Want me to grab your sleeping bag from inside or something?"

I'm supernervous now that it's just Jake and me, especially since he knows about my crush on him, but I manage a tiny laugh. "No, it's okay. I already have your sweatshirt. I can't take all your clothes."

Oh, Meghan, Meghan, Meghan. Why do you say the dumbest things ever? Sheesh. Now it's Jake's turn to blush, and I honestly hadn't even meant anything by that comment. It just . . . came out differently than I'd intended.

What is going on here anyway? Why did Jake want to talk to me outside? I need to get myself under control. I have a best friend to find. Even if we are out of clues and there's less than an hour until my mom arrives, which means Mrs. Guerrero is definitely going to be home very soon, and there basically isn't a thing any of us can do besides wait for that to happen.

Oh. He's looking at me. What? Is it my eyebrow? Did he say something and I was too busy talking to myself in my head to realize it? Because that happens more than I'd like to admit.

But he's staring at me with a friendly look on his face, like we share a secret or something. Right then and there I decide Anna Marie would totally forgive me if I took a ten-minute time-out from the search party. Anna Marie loves love. Not that this is love, but, um, like. Definite strong like. On my part, at least.

Jake's knee bumps against mine (on purpose?), and I break eye contact, jumping a little and yanking my leg away in surprise. *Settle down, Meghan. You don't even know what he wants to talk to you about.*

His voice is so quiet, I have to strain to hear it over the rumble of a lawn mower in a neighbor's yard. "So do you really remember everything from last night?"

I remember Jake sitting across the table from me in the pitch dark, and I remember talking. More talking. Talking for what seemed like forever, even when we were so sleepy and there were long pauses between questions and I'd start to wonder if maybe he'd fallen asleep . . . right before he would finally whisper an answer. I remember him being really easy to talk to, and feeling comfortable. It makes it easier to talk to him now.

"You're not the person we all thought you were," I say.

He looks uncomfortable. "So you do remember our talk?"

"I remember you telling me about how we'd scared you half to death when we snuck into the school last night."

Jake grins. "You got that right!"

I turn my face and pretend to study the tree line at the back of Anna Marie's property until the red in my cheeks go away.

"Tell me again why you were doing that when you didn't have to? You said your dad was talking to the coach? I remember all of last night now, but I think I might have dozed off here and there at the end of our talk."

Jake kicks at the ground with the toe of his shoe. "It's no huge story. With the basketball season wrapping up, my dad wanted to talk to the coach about stuff I could do to get in shape if I wanted to try out for the team next year. It was weird just standing there while they talked about me in Coach's office, so I offered to put the posters up in the gym."

"Oh. But, um, do you really want to play basketball? Did we talk about this, too? I really think I fell asleep for parts. Sorry!"

"No biggie. I might want to play basketball, I don't know. Could be cool, ya know? Dad thinks being part of a team would be good for me, but I'm not sure. Maybe make some new friends or stuff like that." Jake shrugs. "I figured you were dozing off. I might have been here and there too. It was pretty late. Like, three-in-the-morning late."

"Really?" Okay, so I'm actually a tiny bit thrilled at this

information. My parents never ever let me stay up past 12:02, and even that's only on New Year's Eve and only while cuddled between them in their king-size bed watching Times Square on television.

And now I was out until *three o'clock in the morning with a boy.* My mom would have an honest-to-God heart attack right on the spot if she knew that. Either that, or she'd spin herself into orbit. It was at Anna Marie's house and my friends were right inside and nothing at all had happened, but still. Just the idea of it feels so . . . shocking. I've never done anything shocking. In. My. Life.

I bet Jake has. Or actually, now that I know him a little better, maybe not. "You're nice," I say, and he snorts. "How come you don't let people see that?"

Jake sighs. "I do. I try to let everyone see that. I don't even know how I ended up with this stupid reputation. I guess it all has to do with that thing with Anthony Jarrett."

I remember that, too. It is so exceedingly great to have a working memory, let me tell you. Funny the things you take for granted.

Jake is talking about his first week of school in sixth grade. He'd been new, and it was already a little into the year, when everyone had already sorted out who would sit where at lunch and who would play Four Square together at recess. I guess that wouldn't have been easy for a new kid to jump into. My heart clenches. If only I'd been paying more attention back then. I could have been friends with him and helped him figure it all out.

Anthony is a total brownnoser. Teachers love him. All adults love him, basically. Most of the kids, too. Although, for some reason I can't explain, I never have.

On Jake's first day, Anthony had been picking on Cameron Little at recess, as per usual. Cameron lives up (or, well, down) to his last name. Poor guy. Anthony was always teasing him, and no one ever really did anything about it, even though the entire school sat through the anti-bullying assemblies every year. My gut twists a little as I suddenly realize I've never done anything about it. I always figured it was better to keep off Anthony's radar entirely, or so I've managed to convince myself. I'm way too scared of making an enemy out of him.

But Jake hadn't been. Even on his first day at a brand-new school. Maybe because it was his first day and he hadn't yet figured out how much influence Anthony had over . . . well, everyone? But no. Jake's smart. He probably knew pushing Cameron out of the way and getting right up in Anthony's face was a bad idea.

The even worse idea was punching back when Anthony hit him. Of course everyone would believe Anthony when he said Jake had started the whole thing. Principal Wexman is best friends with Anthony's mom. She's even his godmother, or so he claims.

Funny how one small incident (well, not small. It was a fistfight, which was pretty unheard of at our school) could determine Jake's entire reputation from there on out. Poor Jake. He must have been so hurt when no one wanted to hear his side of the story.

Jake uses his toe to give the swing another push and says, "I mean, I'd never hit anyone in my whole entire life. And I haven't since. But after the thing with Anthony, I guess people saw me a certain way. It was better than getting picked on, especially since I was the new kid, so I just sort of let people think what they wanted to think. And, I mean, I do love to skateboard and play guitar and dress how I do—except when my mom makes me wear this stuff for church." Jake gestures to his corduroys. "So, um, yeah. I went along with it. It was easier."

"Oh," I say. I can't really think of what else to add. We rock on the swing quietly for a minute, and then I ask, "But, um, don't you miss having friends?"

"I have friends," Jake says with a laugh. "Geez."

"Oh. I usually see you alone."

"I like being alone. It's quiet."

Jake Ribano isn't anything like I thought he was.

His foot drags along the ground, and he stares at his hands.

I feel like I should probably find something to say, because the silence is sort of awkward, but the problem is, I can't think of anything. It's like my mind is totally blank.

"Um, except . . . ," Jake starts. I glance at him, but he's still staring at his hands in his lap.

"Yeah?" I ask. My heart starts to thump in an uncomfortable way against my rib cage. Is this how like *like* feels?

"Well, I mean, I was just . . ." Jake takes a deep breath, but I can't stop holding mine. He rubs his hands on his corduroys as if they're sweaty, which obviously can't be the case because we're sitting outside and it's pretty cool today. "I was just gonna say that I don't always like to be alone. Sometimes it's kind of nice to have someone to talk to, you know?"

I do. I do know. But is Jake trying to say he wants to have me to talk to? Um, I think maybe he is.

I happen to glance down at Jake's hands, and they're still resting on his pant legs. His legs that are right next to my legs. Where my hands are. Jake follows my eyes to the same spot where our hands are inches apart.

I'm lots of things. I'm smart. I think I'm decently funny and, even though I can admit there are prettier girls in my class, I don't think I'm hideous or anything. Maybe not even with one eyebrow. One thing I'm not, though, is brave. Or at least, I've never been all that brave. I've never tried riding a roller coaster or swimming in the deep end or eating Brussels sprouts. But riding a dirt bike wasn't so scary today, even when I wiped out. Sneaking into school was superscary, but it turned out fine. It was even sort of, well, fun.

Maybe I am brave, and it just took everything that happened this morning to prove it to myself.

I decide I have to (have to) test out this theory before I regret it forever.

I exhale a breath and at the same second move my hand over ever so slightly so that the edge of my pinky finger is right up against the edge of Jake's. I almost jump when our skin touches, but I force myself still. Every single part of me is focused on the tiny spot where our fingers line up. Jake doesn't move, and he doesn't say anything.

I take another deep breath, trying to be quiet about it, and move my pinky again, locking it around Jake's. I steal a sideways glance at him from underneath my eyelashes and see he has a tiny smile on his face. He shocks me by squeezing my finger, and I shock myself by squeezing back. My heart squeezes too.

Forget last night. *Today* is epic.

"You guys! Mrs. G.'s home! We just heard her voice upstairs. And no, we haven't figured out where Anna Marie is." Paige's head sticks out the door, and she blinks a few times when she spots Jake and me sitting so close. Luckily, she proves herself the best kind of friend when she resists commenting. I make a mental note to do something extra-nice for her in thanks.

In a way this is good because I wasn't sure how to talk to Jake all regular and normal now that I'm kind of holding his hand, and Anna Marie's mom being home probably saves me a whole bunch of awkward. Jake untangles his finger from mine and stands, but when he does, he gives me this grin that lets me know he's happy I came outside with him.

I won't lie, I feel pretty glow-y myself.

Except when I realize we really do have to face the music for real this time and confess everything to Mrs. Guerrero. Suddenly not so glow-y after all.

We enter the basement to find Veronica already waiting at the bottom of the stairs. We're like criminals heading off to the firing squad as we trudge slowly up the steps and push open the door. A clattering from the kitchen lets us know just where Mrs. Guerrero is, so we turn in that direction, still walking single file.

I'm in front. Clearly, I didn't think this one through. But here I am, so I might as well get it over with. Seeing as how I'm newly brave and all.

But I don't feel brave one little bit.

I take a deep breath and step through the doorway and into the warm kitchen.

Mrs. Guerrero is sliding a tray of ooey-gooey cinnamon

rolls into the oven. If my stomach hadn't turned to cement, I'm sure it would be rumbling.

"Hey, girls! I was just about to wake you up. Oh, and hello, Jake. I didn't realize you were over. Would you like to join us for a late breakfast?"

She's so sweet and bubbly, just like Anna Marie, that it makes me hurt all over. I can't imagine what her expression will look like when we break our news.

"Um, sure," Jake mumbles.

Paige stands straight. "Uh, Mrs. G., we sort of have to talk to you about something. It might . . . It might be good if you sat down."

"Oh now, whatever it is, don't stress. Honestly, you all look like the world is about to end. Don't worry. There's nothing so precious down in that basement that it can't be replaced."

Except her daughter. My insides feel all mushy, like the guts of a pumpkin. I squeeze my eyes shut for a second and then squeak out, "Actually, it's about Anna Marie."

Mrs. Guerrero's face relaxes even more. "Oh well, in that case, let's get her in here for this. Bug? Anna Marie? C'mere please!" she calls.

I want to tell her she can yell all she wants, but no one will answer.

That is until we hear, "Coming!" from the hallway.

CHAPTER TWENTY

Mystery Solved!

Anna Marie enters the kitchen, a giant grin on her face.

"You guys are lucky you got your butts up here when you did. I was this close to borrowing Max's air horn and heading down to wake you myself. Oh man, Megs. That eyebrow in the sunlight. Yeesh. Should have stuck with Truth!"

We all stare at her. Next to me, Paige's jaw falls open. Veronica's head is cocked, and Jake's forehead wrinkles up.

Anna Marie swipes at her cheek. "What? Do I have something on my face?"

I open and close my mouth a few times. I'm in such shock, I can't form a word. Paige isn't much better, but at least she manages to sputter something that sounds like English. "Wha—? How? I don't—"

Veronica clears her throat and darts a glance at Mrs. Guerrero, who is bent over a new batch of cinnamon rolls.

"Maybe we should talk to Anna Marie in the basement." She doesn't win any points for subtlety, but she has an excellent point.

I don't know why, I don't know how, but Anna Marie is right here in front of us, acting perfectly normal and not at all traumatized. So, clearly, explanations are necessary, but we don't need to let Mrs. Guerrero know anything was ever out of the ordinary. No sense getting in trouble at this point. However, we have to relocate fast because I cannot wait one more second for this to be explained.

"We'll be right back, Mom," Anna Marie says, looking at us like we've gone off the deep end but playing along perfectly.

"Where were you?" I blurt out the second we close the door behind us.

As soon as we get to the bottom of the stairs, she turns to us. "What do you mean, where was I? I left you a note taped right to the mirror. Nobody used the bathroom when they woke up? Wow. That's, like, the first thing I have to do the minute I get out of bed."

I blink rapidly. I should be following this conversation, but it's as if it's happening underwater. Finally I piece together what Anna Marie is saying. "You left us a note?"

Anna Marie nods. "Yup. Taped to the mirror in the bath-room. You really didn't see it?"

Veronica has a hand on her hip. "Must have been too busy gaping at the baby ducklings."

Anna Marie snort-laughs. "Oh man. We were such idiots last night. We have to return those little guys before we get busted."

Anna Marie had left a note. A note none of us noticed. But that's not right. We just cleaned that bathroom. Well, okay, Veronica cleaned it, but surely, she would have noticed. I mean, maybe not, since it's Veronica we're talking about, but the rest of us were in there at different points in the morning, and one of us definitely would have—

Wait a minute. *I* was in there. I was in there first thing in the morning, and I'd done nothing *but* look in that mirror. That was where I'd stared at my missing eyebrow. I'd run to the bathroom the minute Paige had screamed at my face, the minute I'd jumped out of my sleeping bag, the minute—

No. Not the very minute. Because first I'd had to wait for the bathroom door to open. First I'd had to wait for the person in the bathroom before me to leave.

"Max!" I mutter. Paige hears me and catches on immediately.

"Max was in the bathroom when we woke up! And there was no note in sight when we got in there."

Anna Marie rolls her eyes to heaven. "That kid, I swear. Well, at least you're just waking up, so you didn't have time to actually worry about me or anything."

At this I slump down the wall at the base of the stairs

to sit on the floor. Veronica puts her hand on my shoulder and squeezes as Anna Marie looks on, confused. Probably wondering when we've become good enough friends for her to comfort me.

"That's . . . not exactly the case," Paige says, and Anna Marie's eyes grow wide. "We've had a, um, well, a bit of an adventure this morning. Mostly centered around trying to find you."

Anna Marie studies Paige. "Trying to find me? Whoa. Okay, I need the whole story. Start at the beginning."

"You first!" Jake and I speak the same words at the same time.

"Jinx," I say with a grin. Jake smiles. I turn my attention to Anna Marie, who is glancing back and forth between us.

"Where were you?" I ask again.

Anna Marie smiles a satisfied smile. I'm glad to see her looking happy, but I'm dying for her to fill us in. "I was with my dad. So every year on my birthday we do this sunrise hike up to the top of Mount Ellis? But, we, um, we haven't really been seeing eye to eye about this wedding thing. No offense, Veronica."

Veronica shrugs. "No big deal. Although my mom is a lot of fun. She's excellent at *Wheel of Fortune*. And she knits socks."

Anna Marie looks skeptical about both of those things, but

she forces a smile and says, "It's not really about your mom. I'm sure she's great." She addresses us all again. "So anyway, after we finally went to bed last night, I was just lying there in the dark, listening to Veronica snore and realizing it was so late—or early, I guess—that it was pretty close to the time I would have been getting up to hike with my dad. And suddenly I really wished I were doing that. I don't know if it was the hypnosis or what, but it seemed like the best idea ever. So, after a few more minutes, I went upstairs and woke up my mom and she called him to pick me up."

All this time, this entire time, she was safe and sound with a parent. And her other parent knew exactly where she was. All. This. Time.

I want to bang my head on the floor.

"So you and your dad went hiking?" I ask, not because I don't know the answer, of course, but because I need to hear her say it a few times so I can process it.

"It was awesome. With the sun coming up on the trail and making everything sparkle. You should have seen it."

Maybe we could have seen it if we hadn't been so busy breaking into the school and chasing hedgehog floats down hills. But no, that isn't fair. It isn't Anna Marie's fault we didn't get her note. And I'm genuinely happy for her. I know how much Anna Marie has missed her dad since he moved out. This is a good thing.

Veronica says, "My mom can also yodel."

"No offense, Veronica, but that's not really helpful right now," Anna Marie says. I can tell she's fighting back annoyance.

Veronica's shoulders slump, and she hangs her head. "Sorry," she mutters.

I look at Veronica's dejected face, and I can't keep quiet. "Actually, Anna Marie, Veronica has been superhelpful all morning."

"I have?" Veronica asks.

"Of course," Paige says, picking right up for me and smiling at Veronica. A real, genuine smile. "You're the one who did most of the cleaning, even the duck poop in the bathroom. That was pretty awesome."

"More important, you were the one who figured out about Max's YouTube account and how to break the hypnosis," I add.

Anna Marie looks between Paige and me with a stunned expression, and Veronica beams. After a second or two Anna Marie takes a deep breath and faces Veronica. "I guess I owe you a thanks then."

Veronica's grin grows even wider. "Don't mention it. That's just what sisters do, AM."

I can practically hear Anna Marie's teeth grind at both the nickname and the word *sisters*, but to her credit she just shrugs and makes a helpless gesture with her hands. I catch her eye and smile. I know Anna Marie, and I'm betting it won't be that long before she comes around to Veronica.

Jake says, "There are still two things I don't understand. When we first came in, Anna Marie knew Meghan had shaved her eyebrow. And she knew about the ducklings in the tub. But she didn't hear the trigger words, so why isn't she still hypnotized? And why does she remember everything that happened?"

"Huh?" Anna Marie asks, but the rest of us nod along with Jake. He's right. It doesn't make any sense at all.

"There were trigger words to make us snap out of the hypnosis. *New York.* We all heard them when we woke up to 'American Boy' playing, but you weren't home then. So why aren't you still hypnotized?"

Anna Marie's forehead crinkles. She stares off into the distance, and then she snaps her fingers. "The news. When I got into the car, I couldn't stop giggling. My dad said I was acting superweird, so he told me to sit back and try to catch some sleep. He switched on the news, but then I started laughing even harder because there was a story about this teenager who tried to break into his own home by climbing down the chimney and then he got stuck. This was in—"

"New York!" I interrupt. That story was on TV when we were eavesdropping outside the kitchen this morning, trying to find Anna Marie.

"Yup." She grins.

"Okay, but—" Jake begins, and then I interrupt him, too.

"When we woke up, even though we weren't hypnotized anymore, we couldn't remember anything that happened. And then we found out Max had edited this video he took of Madame Mesmer last night to make us forget everything until we heard trigger words. When we saw his YouTube video and heard the trigger, then we did remember. But before that—all morning, actually—we couldn't have told you anything that had happened at the sleepover."

Anna Marie's eyes go all wide again. "Oh wow. Do you think it's because I never went to sleep? Or no, that's not true because I totally crashed out in the car the whole drive home. My dad had to shake me awake. Wait, what was the trigger word?"

"Wordsssss, actually," Jake says. "*Las Vegas.*"

"Not exactly something that comes up in everyday conversation," I add.

Anna Marie lets out this surprised bark kind of sound. "Omigosh! They don't unless you have a dad who tells you in the first five minutes of the hike how glad he is that you called because he was so upset to see how his upcoming marriage was affecting his relationship with me that he and his fiancée decided to elope in Las Vegas to save everyone the awkwardness of a wedding."

Veronica jumps up and down. "Oh, oh! Can we go too?

I wanna see Elvis! You know he's still alive, right?"

Anna Marie smiles. "I don't think they're going through with it anymore. Not after this morning."

"Rats." Veronica looks seriously bummed.

"Well, I guess that's all the mysteries solved," Jake says.

"Not quite," says Paige. "There's one more thing we need to figure out."

Everyone turns to face her as she punches a fist into her palm. "The mystery of what our revenge on Max is going to look like."

We all laugh, but before we have time to entertain delicious scenarios, the doorbell rings. I gasp and look at the clock: 11:55.

My mother is precisely five minutes early to everything. It drives me batty. The doorbell rings again, and from the kitchen upstairs Mrs. Guerrero yells, "Could someone get that please?"

Anna Marie races up the steps and flings open the door. "Hi, Mrs. Alcott."

I swallow. Now that my best friend is safe and sound, I don't want the sleepover to end. I want to sit with everyone and tell Anna Marie about everything that happened while she was off hiking. About Veronica pretending to be a stuffed animal in her room, and about riding the dirt bike and holding hands with Jake. Especially about holding hands with Jake.

I sigh and rise from the floor, brushing off the backs of my legs and butt. "I guess it's time to go." I don't know why I suddenly feel so sad. Anna Marie is home and unharmed, I had a definite moment with Jake, and my parents don't need to find out about any of it. I should be ecstatic. Except I'm anything but. Last night and this morning have been crazy, but they've also been kind of . . . well, fun. Really fun, actually. And now it's over. Just like that.

"I'll get my stuff," I say, looking at the spot in the corner where we'd all neatly stacked our sleeping bags and backpacks and, in one case, cot and camping table.

"I'll grab it," Jake offers.

"I'll help," Veronica says, but Paige yanks on her sleeve. "Um, V, why don't we head upstairs, and you can help me ice the cinnamon rolls? We'll put one in a napkin for Megs to take with her."

Paige is a very, very good friend.

I trail Jake over to my stuff. He picks up my sleeping bag and hands it to me.

I reach for it, but then I remember something. "Oh. Wait. Your sweatshirt." I unzip his hoodie and shrug it off my shoulders, but Jake is shaking his head.

"Oh, uh, that's okay. You can give it back to me next time we hang out. Or keep it. I mean, um, if you want."

Next time we hang out. We're gonna have a "next time." I smile and drop my eyes. "Um, sure. Okay."

Jake stuffs his hands into his pockets. "Okay, so, um, well, this was . . . different."

I can't stop my grin. "You can say that again."

Jake smiles back and moves toward the basement door. "So, I'll see you later?"

"Later," I agree. He slips out the door, and I push his sweatshirt up on my shoulders and hug it tightly around me before clomping up the steps.

When I set foot in the hallway, my mother is chatting with Mrs. Guerrero. She turns in my direction, but before I can take a step, someone grabs my sleeping bag from behind, pulling me up short.

"Not so fast," Anna Marie whispers in my ear. When I spin to face her, Anna Marie pushes a baseball cap onto my head and tugs the brim down low. "This should hide your eyebrow from your mom. For now, at least."

Paige peeks out from behind Anna Marie, holding a napkin oozing delicious, warm, gooey smells, and hands it over. "Sustenance."

I smile. I love that my friends have my back.

They follow me to the front hall, where Mrs. Guerrero is exclaiming, "I really can't believe what angels they were. Usually I have to go downstairs at least five times at these sleepovers to tell everyone to quiet down, but the girls were perfect. I didn't hear a peep out of them all night."

I force myself to stare at the floor to keep from laughing.

CHAPTER TWENTY-ONE

So Long, Farewell . . .

"Well, I'm glad to hear they didn't give you any trouble," my mom says. "And I'm glad I didn't get any late-night calls. Proud of you, Meghan." She pauses and gives me a quick smile. "Now we've got to get going. Paige, would you like a ride?"

"No, thanks. My mom's coming. She's kind of on her own schedule, but at least she's pretty reliable about being unreliable."

Mrs. Guerrero laughs. "You're welcome to stay as long as you like, Paige. Veronica, I already talked to your mother and told her we'd love to have you at Anna Marie's family party tonight, if you'd like to hang here until then."

Veronica beams but then gets all serious. "If Anna Marie's okay with it," she mumbles.

Anna Marie exchanges looks with Paige and me, and we both nod extra hard. She looks at Veronica. "Sure. That'd be cool."

My mom grabs the sleeping bag out of my hands. "Okay,

missy. Let's get going. You have handbell practice, and I don't want to get you there late."

I hug my friends good-bye, including Veronica, and thank Mrs. Guerrero for having me. I turn to follow my mom out the door, but after two steps, I remember something and run back to Anna Marie.

"Happy birthday!" I say, digging the wrapped journal out of my duffel and handing it over. "Something tells me I know exactly what the first entry will be!" I give her another quick hug and, as I do, I whisper in her ear, "I'm glad you're safe."

Anna Marie hugs me back hard.

I join up with Mom and settle myself into the passenger seat. Sitting feels good. Really, really good. I suddenly realize how very little sleep I got the night before, which immediately makes me yawn. We have a ten-minute drive to the church. Maybe I can just catch a second or two of sleep. I let my eyes flutter closed.

My mom always insists on letting the car warm up forever, and today is no exception. She turns to me. "I hope you had fun, because when you get home, your dad and I are going to have a talk with you about why you weren't answering your Ladybug cell this morning. I called you twice, and you didn't answer."

I shrug and put my most innocent expression on my face. "Huh. That's really weird. I didn't even hear it ring on this end."

Not technically a lie.

My mom sighs. "Maybe I dialed wrong. I guess it's time to admit I need to wear my reading glasses. Do you know earlier today I was convinced I saw you at the drive-through of the Dunkin' Donuts? Holding on to some boy on a bike. Is that the craziest thing ever?"

I smile at the memory. "The craziest," I agree.

Also not a lie.

The thought of Jake makes my eyes fly open as my mom puts the car in drive. We'll be passing his house, and what if he's outside and— Yes! He is outside. He's helping his mom roll trash cans to the curb. He catches my eye through the window as our car moves down Anna Marie's driveway and turns onto the street. I give him my best *I like you* smile, and I'm pretty positive his smile says the exact same thing.

"Meghan!"

I jump in my seat. "Um, yeah?"

"I was saying you're going to need to take that hat off when we get to church. It's rude to wear hats inside churches. And didn't you pack any of your own clothes to change into this morning? Why on earth does Anna Marie buy her sweatshirts two sizes too big? And with skulls on them. She seems like such a sweet girl. I can't picture her wearing that. I really can't."

"Actually, Mom, I kind of love this sweatshirt, and it was given to me as a gift, so I think I'm probably gonna wear it a lot from now on."

Whoa. I did not just stand up to my mom like that. I'm a go-along-to-get-along kind of person, just like my dad, especially where my mom is concerned.

But I like Brave Meghan, and I don't want her to go away. Plus, I learned this morning that some things are worth fighting for.

I expect Mom to have something to say on the matter, but she doesn't. Wow. Has she been hypnotized into an understanding parent? Let's just hope this mellow version of Mom is still around when my hat comes off and my unibrow is revealed. I drift off for a minute, imagining how that's all gonna play out.

"Meghan? Meghan!"

"Hmm?"

"I asked how last night was," Mom says.

A series of images flashes through my head: Silly String and "American Boy" and I Never and Paige thinking she was talking to Taylor Swift on the phone and locked schools and ducklings and Japanese janitors and blood that was really paint and band kids and rolling hedgehog floats and YouTube videos and porch swings and porch swings and porch swings. (I prefer that image most of all, so I keep it on a loop in my head.) I swing back to the window and crane my neck to watch the last glimpse of Jake before we turn the corner. He gives me a tiny wave, and I sigh happily.

"Epic, Mom. Last night was epic."

PART THREE

CHAPTER TWENTY-TWO

Revenge Is a Dish Best Served in PJs

> We may be the un-der-dogs,
>
> but we're gonna tromp these mean hedgehogs!
>
> We've got pep and we've got bite!
>
> West Oak's here to fight, fight, fight!
>
> Goooooooo, Warriors!

The eighth-grade cheerleaders are getting the already manic crowd even more fired up as halftime approaches and the score reads: West Oak Warriors: 38, Hillside Heights Havocking Hedgehogs: 36. Our teams are playing again, this time in the state championship.

I put my thumb and pointer finger between my lips and practice the wolf whistle Veronica taught me last week when I tagged along with Anna Marie to the bridal shower for Veronica's mom. It comes out not so much earsplitting as pathetic-sounding, but next to me, Anna Marie just laughs. It's

been three weeks since the Great Anna Marie Disappear-
ance That Wasn't, but I still get a burst of gratitude when I
hear her laugh.

On my other side, Jake bumps my knee against his and
says, "You're getting better. By the end of the game, I'll bet
you have it down!"

My stomach feels like warm, twinkling fireflies are
bumping around inside it. I brush my bangs out of my eyes,
something I'm still getting used to.

True, my mom fuh-reaked out when she spotted my missing eyebrow, but luckily, it happened at handbell rehearsal
and we were in church. I knew my mom would never murder me in front of God. Afterward I was able to convince her
that Paige had tried to teach me how to pluck eyebrows, and
a little more plus a little more plus a little more had ended
up in something so awful, we'd just shaved the whole thing
off in the end. It wasn't the best story ever, and I'm not par-
ticularly proud of lying to my mom, but under the circumstances, what was I supposed to say?

I do feel extra guilty about the fact that I love my new
bangs so much, when I would never have had them if it weren't
for the eyebrow incident. At least my mom wasn't as mad as
I thought she'd be; she even confessed she'd overplucked her
eyebrows into a thin line once when she wasn't much older
than I am. Which was . . . whoa.

I stand and cheer as the Warriors score a three-pointer. West Oak: 41.

Jake smiles at me, and my stomach flip-flops again. It's still a little weird to have him hanging out with us. I can tell the other kids at school are trying to figure out what's going on. I keep catching them looking at me. Although, maybe it's just my new look. Or my new attitude. These last few weeks I've felt freer than ever and ready for more and more and more adventure. Bring it!

Starting with halftime.

I clutch Anna Marie's arm. "It's almost time!"

Anna Marie grins back. "I know!"

A minute later the buzzer sounds, and both teams jog off the court and into the locker rooms. The cheerleaders take center stage and began another cheer.

> West Oak, West Oak, they're a dream.
> That's why we're proud that they're our team!

Half the crowd stomps their feet on the bleachers and applauds. Anna Marie points at the twirling hedgehog mascot taking center stage alongside our West Oak tree mascot (worst costume idea ever, for the record).

"I can't believe that's Veronica!" she says.

"I know! It's crazy," I add.

Jake says, "I still don't completely understand how that happened. She doesn't even go to Hillside." He gestures to Veronica inside the hedgehog mascot costume, swooping her arms in the air to get the Hillside fans riled up. I have to give her credit. Turns out, she doesn't even need to know how to do a roundoff, because she's good. Really, really good.

I lean over to speak into Jake's ear, since the crowd is now screaming at the tops of their lungs. "Don't forget we know a few people over there now. But it gets even better. Wait and see what we have planned."

Anna Marie winks at me and puts a video camera up to her eye.

Just then there's a smattering of pops, like someone let off bottle rockets, and from a side entrance, Hedgie the Hedgehog rolls in on his platform with the entire Hillside Heights marching band surrounding him. They play a fight song, and the giant drums echo through the gymnasium. I can even feel them inside me. *Boom. Boom. Boom.*

Eventually the cheers turn to giggles and pointing as the float turns in a circle and everyone catches sight of a boy standing on the platform next to Hedgie. He's wearing fuzzy My Little Pony pajamas and has pink curlers wound tight in his hair.

The marching band finishes their song, and Flute Girl hops up next to the boy on the hedgehog float, speaking into a microphone. "I'm told you were promised a kiss today, Max. Are you ready for it?"

Max licks his lips. "Am I ever! Paige, where are you, my love?"

A smiling, ponytailed Paige appears underneath the net. One hand is tucked behind her back. Max has a huge smile when he sees her, and he does a fist pump. The audience cheers even louder. This is so perfect.

Paige sashays right up to the float and then crooks her finger to call Max to her. Max hops off, slipping a little on the slick gym floor due to his footy pajamas. He seems utterly unconcerned to be wearing such a ridiculous outfit in front of basically the entire town.

Jake says, "Okay, how did you guys manage to pull this off?"

Anna Marie pipes up from behind her camera, where she's recording everything. "Well, the float part was easy. Paige figured out the weird top hat she found in my basement belonged to the kid with the baton as part of his conductor outfit. So she brought it to the basketball game that afternoon and turned it over. That, plus the fact that by then the band had watched the rest of the YouTube videos on Max's channel by then, trying to figure out what you guys were going on and on about in the Dunkin' Donuts lot, made them really sympathetic. They were happy to help with whatever revenge we cooked up!"

Jake laughs. "Okay, but the pajamas? How the heck did you get him to—"

I let my gaze sweep over the crowd, seeking out one turbaned head in the second row. At exactly the same second, the turban turns, and the woman wearing it stares directly into my eyes, a small smile at the corners of her mouth. Creepy. How does she do that?

I point Madame Mesmer out to Jake. Anna Marie winks at me.

"Never underestimate the power of suggestion," I say smugly.

In center court, Paige approaches Max. He rubs his hands together and then closes his eyes and puckers his lips, tilting his head in an exaggerated plant-one-on-me gesture.

Paige steps right up to him and brings her face close to his, but at the very last second, her hand comes out from behind her back, and Max ends up placing his lips right up against the hard duckling bill of Waddleworth. The entire audience screams and cheers and laughs. Max's eyes fly open, and he blinks in confusion.

Paige curtsies to the crowd, then grabs Max by the hand and leads him out of the gym to catcalls and whistles. I try my wolf whistle again, and it isn't half bad this time.

Anna Marie, Jake, and I make our way down the bleacher stairs to find Paige. When we reach the bottom, a giant hedgehog costume comes barreling toward us and catches me in a hug.

"You guys! Guess what." Only it sounds like, "Oof eyes. Essa whaa," through the hedgehog costume.

Anna Marie lifts the heavy head just enough so Veronica's lips appear, before laughing and asking, "What?"

The lips smile. "So I asked my mom today, and she said she's totally cool with it."

Nothing is ever black-and-white with Veronica. Now that I know it's just how she is, I'm more amused than annoyed. But I still have to ask, "Cool with what, Veronica?"

Now the lips curl. "Oh. Oops. Sorry. Cool with me inviting you, Anna Marie, and Paige over next weekend."

Veronica bounces up and down in her costume before adding:

"For a sleepover!"

ACKNOWLEDGMENTS

First and biggest thanks to my editor, Amy Cloud. Your joyfulness and energy is surpassed only by your mad skillz with the editing pen. I'm yours as long as you'll have me, Princess Warrior!

Everyone at Simon & Schuster, from the sales reps to the publicity and marketing teams to the production team, who work so hard to connect every book with the right readers: You are not unappreciated! Special shout-outs to Teresa Ronquillo, Faye Bi, Kaitlin Severini, Laura Lyn DiSiena, Lucy Truman, and Kayley Hoffman.

Giant thanks to my agent, Holly Root, for making me even more excited to write this book. When I first pitched this idea to you, your e-mail back to me read (and I quote) "Holy heck-weasels, you have to write this!" (Of course, I had to steal your phrase for Meghan.) Thanks for that and all the many other e-mails that make me LOL.

Alison Cherry, Dee Romito, and Gail Nall—you guys always

get lumped together in my acknowledgments, but without each of your individual comments, this book would not exist. Dana Alison Levy and Ronni Arno, you are also the very bestest of the best! I would not want to be in this industry without any of you. Truly.

A special thank-you to Nick Sicurella for introducing me to the sport of unicycle floor hockey (which I will never attempt myself). To Jack, Ben, and Caroline, who ask to host sleepovers far too often, and to John, who stays awake with me to police them, I love you guys *thismuch*.

And most of all, to those of you who read my books: I am humbled and grateful and full of love for all of you who allow me to continue to do something I adore so much. Thank you!

IF YOU LIKED *THE SLEEPOVER,*
TURN THE PAGE TO READ CHAPTER ONE OF
BEST. NIGHT. EVER.

BEST. NIGHT. EVER.

A STORY TOLD FROM SEVEN POINTS OF VIEW

WRITTEN BY RACHELE ALPINE, RONNI ARNO, ALISON CHERRY,
STEPHANIE FARIS, JEN MALONE, GAIL NALL, AND DEE ROMITO

CARMEN {6:00 P.M.}

USUALLY LYNNFIELD MIDDLE SCHOOL'S GYM smells like sweaty socks and armpits.

But tonight, everything is different.

Tonight, the gym smells like perfume, hairspray, and the pizza that everyone devoured right away. And instead of getting pelted in the face during a vicious game of dodgeball or doing a million jumping jacks, my friends and I are about to make history when we perform our band's hit song, "Hear Us Roar."

The room buzzes with excitement. Our classmates gather at the makeshift stage the drama club constructed, some pushing to get as close as possible, others taking selfies in front of the giant sign the decorating committee hung up with our name, Heart Grenade, written across it.

Suddenly the room goes dark and the audience erupts in cheers. This is it. Our moment!

A single spotlight turns on, illuminating me.

I look out into the crowd and soak up the moment as my classmates' shouts wash over me. I picture myself as they might. My long black hair is flat-ironed sleek and shiny, and the light from above draws attention to my red streaks. My satin dress poofs out at the bottom, and the short white leather jacket looks amazing over it. I have on Mom's vintage biker boots with the big silver buckles, and hot pink tights add the perfect touch. I'm rocker cute, as my best friend, Tess, likes to say.

"Hello, Lynnfield Middle School!" I yell into the microphone. The sound of my voice sweeps through the gym. "We're Heart Grenade, and we're ready to rock!"

Tess starts playing the drums, Faith comes in on the bass, and as Claudia launches into her signature guitar riff, the lights go up over the whole band, and our classmates go wild.

I open my mouth to start singing . . . and something soft smacks me in the head.

"Ouch!"

And just like that I'm jolted out of the best daydream ever and back into the worst reality ever. Because instead of being in the middle school gym performing with Heart Grenade like I'm supposed to be tonight, I'm surrounded by beige-and-maroon-striped wallpaper in a very tiny and very crowded hotel room with my family.

My eyes land on my ten-year-old brother, Lucas. He's dressed in a gray suit that's too short for him, and his dark hair is all spiky, even though Mom told him it would be really nice if he just combed it straight. But his appearance isn't what I care about; it's what is in his hands. He's holding Pandy, my bear that I *may* still sleep with, although I'd never admit that to anyone. He dances around me and dangles Pandy in front of my face.

I yank her away from him. "Get your grubby hands off of my bear."

"Gladly. I've got some reading to do anyway." Lucas pulls my diary from under his pillow on the bed.

"Give me that!" I reach to grab the notebook with the hand that isn't holding Pandy, but he pulls it away from me. I have no idea how the little sneak got hold of it, since I packed it deep down into my duffel bag, but there's no way I'm letting him see what's inside. He'd never let me live down the pages I filled about how cute my bandmate Claudia's brother is.

"Mooooom," I yell, but she waves a hand at me. She's talking on the phone in rapid-fire Spanish to my aunt Sonia, or "the mother of the bride," as everyone keeps saying, and is trying to convince her that something to do with the flowers is going to be all right. But meanwhile, this diary situation most certainly is not going to turn out all right.

I tackle Lucas and thankfully wrestle the notebook away

from him, but not before getting an elbow to the gut and a knee to my head.

"You'd better sleep with one eye open," I warn him. "I'm not going to forget this."

"Ohhhh, I'm so scared," he replies and rolls his eyes.

"You look like Christmas," my seven-year-old brother, Alex, says, and my attention shifts to him. Yep, I have two younger brothers. Two *annoying* little brothers. It's pretty much the worst ever.

"Christmas?" This is March; that holiday is long gone.

"Yep, with that green dress and those awful red streaks you put in your hair, you make me want to watch *Rudolph* and hang ornaments on the tree."

"Whatever! You're the ridiculous one, with your purple tie and sweater vest," I say.

"If you say so, Jolly Old Saint Nick."

"I don't look like Christmas," I tell him, but I walk over to the mirror. The girl who stares back at me isn't happy at all. Instead of the cute black dress I gazed at every time we went to the mall, the one I'd planned to buy for our big concert, I have on a junior bridesmaid dress that's about as pretty as a pillowcase. It's made of some stretchy fabric that bunches up around my waist and digs into my armpits. And it's green. Not the cute emerald green or Kelly green that all the celebrities wear these days, but bright elf green. My brothers are right; with the red streaks in my hair, I'm ready to deck the halls and have myself a merry little Christmas.

"I'm suddenly in the mood for milk and cookies," Lucas says, coming up behind me.

"That's it," I announce. "I refuse to wear this!"

I go to my suitcase and pull out my jeans with the rhinestones that I wore on the drive here because right now, no dress is better than wearing this one. I try to reach behind and unzip the offending dress, so I'll at least look the part of the lead singer even if I'm not rocking out with everyone back at school.

"Not a chance," Mom says. The phone is still up against her ear, so I pray maybe she's talking to my aunt instead of me. "You're not putting that on," she says, crushing all my hopes.

"But why not? The ceremony is over, and we took a million pictures of me in this awful thing. Can't I wear these now?"

"You're wearing the dress your cousin picked out for you. It's your cousin's night, so you'll do what makes her happy."

What about what makes me *happy? It was supposed to be my night,* I want to say, but it's no use trying to convince Mom. I can tell from the glare she gives me that I won't win this argument.

I try a different approach and decide to talk to Dad instead. He's always the easier one to convince, especially when it involves ice cream before dinner or staying up past my bedtime. Dad's a sucker for my sad face, and sticking out my bottom lip and looking especially pathetic always seals the deal.

I've studied the bus maps, and even though we are almost three hours from home, if I take the six thirty p.m. bus, I might make it back so I can sing with the band. Imagine everyone's surprise and delight if I showed up. They'd be so excited, especially since they were all upset when I broke the news that my parents were making me go to this wedding. It was awful; we all cried a little bit. Well, except Genevieve, who got really, really quiet. She's probably thrilled to be in the spotlight since she only joined a month ago as a backup singer and now she gets to take my spot in the lead.

"Dad, what do you think about taking me to the bus station before you all go to the reception? I can go home early, sing with the band, and stay with Tess."

"Yeah, and he can also drop me off at the airport for a flight to Disney World," Alex says, and I want to scream. "There's no way you're going to be allowed to ride the bus alone."

"Stay out of this," I snap.

"He's right," Dad says. He doesn't even take his eyes off the TV, and I can't believe he's abandoning me instead of being my ally. "That's too dangerous. And besides, you know how excited Mom is for us to spend family time together."

"This is so unfair. It's Heart Grenade's big night. We worked so hard to win the Battle of the Bands at the mall, and now I can't claim our prize."

"We've been over this already, Carmen. You made a commitment to be in your cousin's wedding," Mom says. She's finally hung up the phone, probably so she can direct all her attention toward continuing to ruin my night.

"But that was before we won." I try to reason with her. "When am I ever going to be on TV again?"

"You'll survive," Mom says.

But I'm really not sure I will. Our local station is broadcasting Heart Grenade's concert to everyone during the evening news, and I won't be a part of it.

"You don't understand. Anyone could be watching. I'm pretty sure Taylor Swift got discovered in a similar way."

"And I also bet that she went to all her family weddings," Mom says. She touches up her bright red lipstick in the mirror and doesn't seem to care at all that my life is ending. "It's good to spend time as a family."

"Well, you got your wish," I say.

"How about you try to have fun? You might even find that being at this wedding isn't so awful, *mi pajarita*."

She tries to pull me into a hug that I most definitely do not want.

I wiggle out of it and back away. "Fun? You don't understand anything! When I have daughters, I'm always going to listen to them and make sure I support everything they want to do."

I huff and puff all the way to the bathroom to make sure everyone knows how mad I am. I slam the door and sit on the edge of the bathtub.

This is a million times more horrible than I'd imagined. I pull out my cell phone and send a text to Tess.

Help! Emergency! Come save me STAT!!! This is a tragedy! I need to be with all of you!

I wait for her to reply and wish that she really could come to save me. But when you're stuck an entire state away in a hotel room, that's pretty much impossible.

Someone bangs on the door.

"Time's up, Mrs. Claus. I need to get in there," Alex yells.

I turn on the water in the tub full blast to drown him out, scroll through my Instagram feed, and torture myself with picture after picture of everyone getting ready for the dance. I burst out laughing at a picture from earlier in the afternoon of my classmate (and Tess's mortal enemy) Mariah with a green face mask on and the caption, *Do you all like my makeup for the dance? Perfect, right?!* I scroll through and pause on a cartoon one of my classmates drew of Heart Grenade's logo. *Can't wait to hear my favorite band live* is written on the bottom.

"My life is over!" I wail.

"Carmen, open up right now! This isn't funny," Lucas whines. "I drank two cans of soda and need to use the bathroom."

"Should've thought about that before you made fun of my dress."

I hear Dad yell something with my name in it, so I know it's only a matter of time before he comes over and tells me to open the door.

I grab for my phone as it lights up, telling me I have a text.

Except it isn't from Tess.

It's from Genevieve.

THE Genevieve, who is taking my place tonight as lead singer.

A.k.a. . . . the last person in the world I want to hear from.

Hope the wedding is fun. Wish you were here!

I feel a little better. At least the band is thinking of me.

I'm about to respond when another message from her pops up on the screen.

Any last-minute advice?

Seriously? She's asking me for advice? That's like kicking someone when they're down.

I don't want to give her advice; I want to be up there onstage. I fight back tears while Lucas continues to pound on the door and Alex sings Christmas carols. And his song choice couldn't be better, because it's going to be a "Silent Night" for me as the lead singer of Heart Grenade.

Looking for another great book?
Find it
IN THE MIDDLE.

Fun, fantastic books for kids
in the in-be**TWEEN** age.

IntheMiddleBooks.com

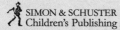

New mystery. New suspense. New danger.

Nancy Drew
DIARIES™

BY CAROLYN KEENE